BILLION DOLLAR BRACKET

DREW BRIDGES

BQB

Virginia

Published in the United States by BQB Publishing
(an imprint of Boutique of Quality Books Publishing, Inc.)
www.bqbpublishing.com

Printed in the United States of America

ISBN 978-1-945448-89-8 (p)
ISBN 978-1-945448-90-4 (e)

Library of Congress Control Number: 2020945336

Book design by Robin Krauss, www.bookformatters.com
Cover design by Rebecca Lown, www.rebeccalowndesign.com

First editor: Caleb Guard
Second editor: Andrea Berns

PRAISE FOR BILLION DOLLAR BRACKET AND DREW BRIDGES

"By the end of the first page, I was hooked. *Billion Dollar Bracket* tells a story about intelligence, big money, mental illness, trust, diversity, and yes, basketball. A fascinating story."

– Tina Zion, Author, Lecturer

"This book was tailor-made for me, telling the stories of many actors in the drama, with surprises every few chapters. In one of the multiple plot lines, Drew Bridges gives the reader a window into what it means for young athletes to deal with the competing demands of college sports. As a coach, I've lived parts of this story."

– Larry Marciniak, Assistant Basketball Coach
at two different high schools and two different
colleges in over 15 consecutive seasons

"Drew Bridges keeps you on the edge of your stadium seat as you follow the bouncing ball from the hardwood courts, through the genius of the world of social media, and into the lives of those who embrace the March Madness of NCAA basketball. From the 'war room' of a Las Vegas gaming contest, to a small, rural southern university, every chapter changes the game. Who comes out a winner, and who is marked the loser, should come as a big surprise."

– William R. Finger, author of
The Crane Dance: Taking Flight in Midlife

"In this new novel by Drew Bridges there's a lot to like: razor-sharp insights into the worlds of sports and mathematical probabilities, compelling characters, and a plot that keeps you turning the pages. This is more than a book about basketball. I give it my hearty recommendation.

– Lucy Adkins, co-author of *Writing in Community* and *The Fire Inside* (soon to be released)

"An intriguing story about hidden motives in the ultimate betting pool. It's the NCAA basketball bracket contest on steroids. Odds are you will find *Billion Dollar Bracket* a winner.

– Robert Moseley, author of *Choker*

CONTENTS

THE PITCH

"Could I interest you in a proposal that will earn you the easiest $5M you will ever make—no risk—with only a few months of a modest investment of your time?" She tried out various facial expressions and body postures, seeking a verbal and visual punch to the final version of her sales pitch. The mirror gave little feedback.

Still not satisfied with her opening line that she had modified and practiced hundreds of times, Sinclair Dane, head of Dane Statistics, Inc., brushed a piece of lint from the knee of her navy blue pantsuit and turned to answer the ding-dong sound of her office front door. Her first guest had arrived. She took a deep breath as she walked to the door to welcome a much older man who stood a head shorter than her five feet and eight inches. Well indoctrinated in all the subtle mannerisms designed to avoid the appearance of challenging men in positions of power, she felt herself instinctively lower her shoulders and head as she greeted him.

"It's good to see you, Mr. Alinsky; thank you for coming." She felt relieved to hear her voice come out strong but relaxed, neither hurried nor girlish.

"Name's Alinsky, not 'Mister' Alinsky. Just Alinsky. Would you call Prince 'Mister' Prince? You don't call Madonna 'Miss' Madonna, do you? It's just Alinsky."

Forcing herself not to smile or otherwise react to the signature grumpiness of one of Las Vegas's legendary casino owners, Sinclair silently congratulated herself for anticipating how this first meeting would start. She had done her research on his life, his interests, and his accomplishments. Confident that she knew more about him than he knew about her, she believed she could use this information to her advantage. She knew that even after his retirement a decade ago, Alinsky still maintained a high social profile and was sought out regularly by entrepreneurs, despite what some considered a well-manicured rough edge.

The simultaneous arrival of her two other guests cut their greeting short. Rod Browning of Browning Advertising Group came in first, followed by Marilyn Seale, a woman making a name for herself locally with workshops and seminars about social media marketing.

Rod Browning wore a sweat suit and sneakers, and carried no briefcase or even a pen or pencil. Sinclair read this as a sign of minimal interest in the purpose of the meeting. Marilyn Seale, on the other hand, was the picture of a dressed-for-success professional woman. Her thin, leather briefcase plus an easily readable name tag highlighting her business logo accented her long-skirted business look of clearly more style and expense than Sinclair owned.

The necessary introductions took place while everyone walked a short distance to a separate conference room. They took seats around a table that filled up most of the space in the room. The walls displayed few decorations, mostly generic landscapes, photography, and a map of the city of Las Vegas. The room had an unused look to it, chairs showing no wear, and no work papers or documents lay on the table or elsewhere in the room. Alinsky adjusted his chair, lifting the seat to a higher position and moving it a short distance away from where the others were seated. He tugged on the lapels of his vested, gray suit, accessorized with a purple handkerchief in the appropriate pocket, his facial expression suggesting some undeclared irritation or impatience.

Following a minimal amount of small-talk, Sinclair Dane opened a black, leather-bound folder and positioned a pen and writing pad in front of her. The group caught the cue that it was time to start the meeting and grew silent. Alinsky reached into his coat pocket and pulled out a checkbook-sized notepad while Marilyn Seale opened her briefcase to retrieve a small laptop computer, encased in leather that matched her other business tools.

"Are you interested in a proposal to make you the easiest $5M you will ever make?" Sinclair opened. "And would it be even more interesting if I said that $5M could grow to an attractive multiple of that number if we are successful in what I am about to propose?"

All three looked at her without speaking. Their expressions conveyed polite skepticism. They traded quick glances with each other. After a few seconds of silence, Alinsky grunted out, "We're listening." Marilyn Seale typed a short note into her computer.

Sinclair continued, "I'm going to assume that since you came here, you have read the information about my background, but just for the record, I'm ten years out of MIT where I studied statistics with an emphasis on probability theory. Since graduation, I've been a good girl—or as I would rather say, a good soldier—for two organizations everybody knows. Now I have my own company, and I have an idea. My idea seizes the reality that making money betting on NCAA basketball is an underrealized revenue-generating opportunity."

"Not an entirely new idea," growled Alinsky, revealing, if not exaggerating, a Jersey accent. "But go on."

Sinclair felt encouraged. One version of her expectations for this meeting had Alinsky walking out at this point. He was known to dismiss other business petitioners that quickly, but the man was actually listening to her.

For the next five minutes, Sinclair Dane described in detail her plan to offer a $1B prize for a contest, the purpose of which would be predicting the winners in every game of the NCAA basketball tournament. She carefully reviewed the numbers related to the probability of someone actually producing a perfect bracket, then followed up with an estimate of the revenue from several small entry fee options. Making assumptions from those numbers, she projected a payout of $5M profit for each of the four people in the room.

She ended the opening by repeating, in a somewhat dramatic fashion, the numbers she had polished as her hook. "The odds of someone successfully predicting the outcome of all the games for a tournament involving sixty-eight teams is nine quintillion to one. That's a nine with sixteen zeroes . . . to one."

Marilyn Seale softly posed a question: "But what if someone does come up with a perfect bracket? Where do you get $1B? I mean, I've heard that Warren Buffet did this kind of thing, but no one in this room is—"

Sinclair Dane interrupted her guest. "I can run those probability numbers by you again if I need to, but is the probability zero? No. There is risk here. But here is more about my reward side of this . . . " She stood up, walked to the end of the room, and pulled down a cloth cover from a large easel. A poster displayed the words that accompanied a colorful logo: "Dane Statistics, Inc., Statistician to the Odds Makers."

"If I am right about what I have told you, and what I have *yet* to tell you"—she spoke slowly for dramatic effect, punching the word "yet" to build interest—"then this will be how I build the agency I want. I'll tell you my vision for this later, if you're interested. But if I'm wrong about the numbers, I'll be teaching remedial math at a community college. That's my risk. We can structure this so that your risk is zero, and I take all the risk. You can be just someone who is contracting with me. That way I take the risk and a larger share of the reward. Or you can share the—very low—risk and the greater payoff."

Sinclair returned to her seat without hurry and looked down at her hands resting on the table. She hoped they saw that her fingers did not tremble. Then she spoke, looking up quickly, "But I'm not wrong. And now I have told you the basic outline of how you can walk away with $5M each for simply doing what you already do, no money down, just a little more work in the months of February and March. And with the odds in your favor of nine quintillion to one. So, are you ready to hear how that $5M might grow to a handsome multiple of that number?"

"I doubt this is legal," Rod Browning put in. "I mean, I'm assuming you don't have $1B to pay if you are wrong." He pushed his seat back and reached down to tighten the laces of his running shoes. Sinclair expected him to leave soon. Marilyn Seale started to type, then stopped, sighed, and looked at her hands without speaking, avoiding all eye contact.

Sinclair paused, then stood and paced as she replied, "Legal? Yes, technically speaking. I have good counsel on this. I accept their guidance that we can do it in a way that it skirts all the laws on the books. We start and register it offshore. I'll tell you exactly where that is when all the ink is dry. Furthermore, we can set it up online in a manner so that it's 'not really gambling.'" She made the air quotation sign with her fingers. "It's a contest, and they pay a processing fee of two dollars, and if they click on the 'I accept' button like everyone always does. And they have to click on the accept button if they want a chance to win $1B . . . and . . . and if what they are accepting is written right, we're home free. And here's the clincher—we offer them a way to enter free, but with a lot more trouble, print the bracket, fill it out by hand, maybe even get it notarized. But with things like PayPal, everyone's going to just make a few clicks on whatever device they have and pay the two dollars."

She paused to gauge the reaction of those in the room, then continued, "But even so, you have to accept the reality that it's a clean process as long as nobody wins. If someone does, and wants $1B from us, it honestly does get a bit murky. That would put us in uncharted waters."

Sinclair took a sip of water from a glass on the table and looked at each of the others in turn. She thought she still saw doubt, and she spoke to acknowledge it, to assure them she had really thought the process through, "But here's the other thing. What I'm getting ready to describe is legal now. It probably won't be next year if it works. Not far from here, a couple of hotshot state attorneys general are trying to make a name for themselves, and they'd love to jump on this. Or if it works and it stays legal, everybody will be doing it next year. So, we have one shot at this. And if it doesn't work, and someone comes up with a perfect bracket, we can't pay."

Realizing her voice was becoming strident, she forced herself to slow down and be calm. She took another drink of water. She looked at the others; they all remained silent, but she was still hopeful. Alinsky was still in the room. He was the key to moving forward. Without him and his knowledge of gaming and gaming law, it would be difficult to see the process through.

After a deep breath, Sinclair resumed, "And the fact that it's not technically illegal won't matter. We could have an injured party and a lawsuit could come. So, it all comes down to this: do you like the odds of nine quintillion to one? If you do, then let me ask you again: do you want to hear more details about how we're going to do this? To get 35 million people to each send us $2. And do you want to hear about your part in it? It's January. March will be here before you know it."

All three guests leaned back, settling into their seats. Alinsky spoke, "I assume you brought doughnuts?"

After searching the faces of the others, Rod Browning pulled his chair back up to the table and asked Marilyn Seale if he could borrow a piece of paper, adding that he had left his cell phone in his car. Sinclair smiled, reached across the table, and slid a pen into his hand.

2

THE PLAN

Sinclair Dane left her office after the meeting with a mixture of excitement, fear, and worry. Excitement because the meeting accomplished all and more than she had hoped. Alinsky at one point had walked out saying he would not be a party to a fraud, but during the fifteen minutes he was gone, he sat just outside in his 1963 Lincoln Continental and made some phone calls. He then dramatically burst back in the room, just as Sinclair's two other guests had stood up to leave, telling everyone to sit back down, speaking and gesturing with the comportment of someone who was accustomed to giving orders.

Alinsky poked his chest with his finger and paced around the room, his previously raspy voice now booming with an operatic tone. "I've got a plan. This can work! It's a casino in a computer, this little scheme you've hatched. And I know casinos. I don't know computers, but people who do know computers are a dime a dozen."

Marilyn and Rod at first looked startled as Alinsky strutted around the room, but he soon calmed himself, and in short order he had described for them a plan for a complex reinsurance scheme whereby a group of casino owners and a reinsurance company would guarantee the $1B payment if it came to that.

"This is what I do," Alinsky told them as punctuation to his plan. "I talk numbers and odds; people believe in numbers and odds. And when it's me that's talking numbers and odds, they listen."

The three others were in equal measure impressed and amused when Alinsky spoke. He again had become animated, continued to punch his chest with his finger each time he referred to himself, gesturing wildly with both hands, his face bursting with expression that swung from anger to glee. But they listened. They knew he was right.

Then Alinsky changed his tone and quietly presented the more complicated part of the plan, the cost of the arrangement to guarantee $1B payout, if it came to that. Reinsurance would not come cheap. Alinsky promised that he would step up with the advance six figures needed for the reinsurance expense, but only if he got paid first as soon as the money came rolling in.

Sinclair Dane saw her anticipated payday grow smaller with all the other players now involved, but she fought the urge to argue with Alinsky. She knew she could not control everything. She held to confidence in her plan. Most importantly, she remained convinced that no one could produce a perfect bracket, but if someone did win the $1B, it could be paid.

Alinsky then reviewed the only remaining risk, that if there were a perfect bracket, no one would make any money from the overall scheme. All revenues from entries would also go to the guarantor of the $1B payout. Everyone would lose, except the genius that beat the odds and picked a perfect bracket.

Sinclair Dane grew further concerned when Alinsky presented an additional element of the reinsurance scheme, having to do with a lien on her property. The backers Alinsky brought in would want all the key participants to put something at risk. She could lose her house or her office; she could choose which of the two she wanted to make vulnerable. She had to assign risk to some personal property. She wondered if Alinsky was testing her, maybe even trying to steal her idea if she did not put "skin in the game." Her mind raced behind a face that betrayed little emotion, as she tried to fully understand and accept this relationship with Alinsky. She knew that she needed him. Yet seeing his power and influence in the world of money and his ability to make deals happen, deep down she wondered if she could trust him. She thought back to another time in a board room where a mentor had taken more than one of her ideas—and the credit for them.

Rod Browning and Marilyn Seale refused to put assets at risk, but remained in the partnership under a different sort of contract with a reduced percentage share of the profits. Alinsky took over what they gave up, so he stood as the potential big winner. Toward the end of the meeting he gave them all a list of things for each of them to accomplish in order to make the back-up plan a reality. Just before he left, he turned to Rod and Marilyn and gave them an order, and then repeated it: Whatever marketing and advertising they were cooking up could not mention, name, or in any way refer to the National Collegiate Athletic Association, or use its acronym.

He pointed his finger at each of them in turn as he emphasized, "You do not want the NCAA on your case about this. You can say all you want about basketball brackets and colleges, but not the NCAA." Sinclair wondered what kinds of history Alinsky had with the NCAA, but she felt it was beyond information she needed or wanted for now.

Rod Browning started to ask for more information about why the NCAA was to be feared, but Alinsky stopped him and repeated, "If you get me started on that now, I'll never finish. I don't have time now. Just put it into your little computers and your brains that those four letters, N-C-A-A, are not in your vocabulary. And I mean it. Okay? Conversation over!"

After saying goodbye to Sinclair, Rod and Marilyn left the

meeting together and stood outside by her car reviewing what had just taken place.

"I'm a little stunned, I must say," Marilyn began. "I had no idea what I was coming here for."

Rod answered, "Ditto for me. I have no idea why I was asked. There's lots of people at my level in the ad industry. Do you think we should do this? Are we getting into something stupid?"

"Oh, I'm not thinking about backing out," Marilyn shot back energetically. "We might just have stumbled into something special, something unique. I know about Alinsky. He's not a crook, but I'll sure run this by my lawyer. I'll let you know what she says."

Sinclair stood alone at her front door and watched them all leave. Getting into her car, she allowed herself a chuckle about how much Alinsky really did look like an aging Danny DeVito, and she silently gave thanks that no one had made a comment about that part of his appearance. References to Danny DeVito were one of several things guaranteed to send the casino mogul into a rage.

Still, she asked herself out loud whether this contest was a good idea after all. She fought her fear by returning to the numbers. If every person in the United States filled out a bracket, there would be one winner in four hundred years. Only if it came in the first year would that be a problem. The previous year, more than 70 million people had filled out brackets in places as small as the office pool and as large as the ESPN website. She held to her belief that at least half that number would pay a two dollar entry fee. That many entries would be profits sufficient to earn even more than the $5M she dreamed about. She smiled and said softly to herself, "So, this is what it feels like to push your own idea without having to beg a board or CEO. I like it."

As she drove away, other worries slowly took over. She was late for the regular weekly meeting time with her mother, Lillian. She gunned her fifteen-year-old Mercedes toward downtown Las Vegas and made her way to East Twain Avenue near the corner of Swenson Street. This was where she would find her mother, either there or farther east or south near Katie Street. Occasionally, she could be found in the nearby Dollar Tree or around the corner from Walgreens, where she sometimes "borrowed" shopping carts to carry all her possessions. Her mother lived homeless and defied all attempts to convince her to live in a real house or apartment. For close to a decade, Lillian Dane had called the streets of Las Vegas her real home.

Sinclair spotted her mother walking slowly along Katie Street, pushing a shopping cart piled high with clothes and various found items. Lillian Dane wore a heavy overcoat despite the typically temperate January day in Las Vegas. Sinclair slowed the car, drove beside her mother, and called out to her through the open car window.

In response to Sinclair's greeting, the older woman answered, "I hear you say who you are and what you want, but how do I know who you really are and what you really want?" Sinclair thought to herself that, today, her mother's response conveyed less fear and carried a softer rejection than the usual ritual of mother ignoring daughter, then mother acknowledging her presence but challenging her identity.

"Hey, Mom; it's great to see you. You look fabulous. I have some money for you." Daughter had learned the right tone of voice along with the tangible enticement that would eventually lead to the two of them finding a safe place to park the car, keeping the shopping cart in view beside the front passenger seat so that they could sit together for a short period of time and talk.

Even in January, greenery and some flowering plants grew in the medians and in front of businesses and homes. A place where flowers were in bloom on the street often proved an acceptable place for conversation. Sinclair eased the car into a diagonal parking space with no car on either side. After entering the front seat, Sinclair's mother scanned both the back seat and the area around the car. She craned her neck first in one direction and then the other, rechecking several times. After several minutes, she gave approval for where the car was parked.

The conversation evolved as usual, not entirely scripted, but the same items were always included. "I still have the apartment rented for you, Mom. You know, Hampton. It's just around the corner. And here's a few more of those labels for your stuff. Got your name printed on them. See? Your name. 'Lillian.'"

"I like the labels, but I don't live there," her mother replied in a monotone, brushing the few stray strands of hair back in place from her otherwise neatly groomed brown but graying hair. Mother then glanced at daughter, opened her mouth to speak, but changed her mind and looked away.

"I know you don't go there, Mom, but I'll always keep it up for you, and anytime you want to move in, it's there. I go there a couple of times a month to make sure it's clean and safe and there's food in the fridge that won't spoil." Sinclair no longer felt she was dying inside whenever she repeated those words, but her hope that her mother would eventually accept the apartment slipped a little each time she said it.

"I'm glad you have a nice apartment, honey. You always were such a nice, sweet, clean girl. You were never that pretty, not like your mother, but that never seemed to hold you back. Except in the husband thing." The remnants of a smile crossed her mother's lips, and the older woman seemed to settle back into her seat.

Sinclair had long made peace with her mother's blunt appraisal of her looks. Such statements no longer stung like they once did. Sinclair also always knew when the visit was coming to an end.

Lillian Dane would relax and the fear in her eyes would vanish. For just a few moments, they would share a sense of togetherness that could have been any mother and daughter sitting together talking about life. Sinclair would talk about her work, and her mother would reveal just a little about her life on the streets.

The personal warmth and intimacy would soon enough appear to frighten the older woman, and Sinclair knew that to express anything negative, any anger, impatience, or disappointment would speed her mother's exit from the car and make the next visit more uncomfortable. So, she watched her mother excuse herself and leave. She always handed her a few folded twenty dollar bills as a last gesture of kindness and hope.

Sinclair Dane came to accept and value that her mother seemed happy and energized after every visit. She reassured herself that what she was doing was all that could be done, and this brought some peace. But her thoughts eventually returned to some version of asking the same question: *Is that same crazy-making time bomb ticking in my own head?* Or would she escape the curse of madness that transformed her mother from a successful woman—socially refined, academically acclaimed—into who she was now? She knew that her mother was not the only woman in her family tree who spent time in mental facilities of various sorts. Sinclair wondered how much time remained for her to build her own safety net.

3

BRACKETOLOGY

Two months later, and three-fourths of a continent east of Sinclair Dane's meeting with her new business partners, Dr. Lewis Cusac walked cautiously into the room of his classroom teaching assignment. Competing emotions of apprehension and excitement came with his very different role at his new school, Gardner-Webb University in Boiling Springs, North Carolina. Feeling tired and older than his sixty years of age, he surveyed the classroom filled with students. His first impression was that they looked larger and more physically fit than a typical class, clearly the athletes he was told would populate his class. He noted silently with surprise that half of the class was female.

A tall woman with big arms in the front row noticed the Duke University logo on his briefcase and quipped, "Better not flash that Duke thing around here, especially if we play them in the Sweet Sixteen." Not a sports fan, Cusac did not understand the reference, but he put his briefcase under the desk and smiled at her. He removed his tan jacket and loosened his necktie, presenting a rumpled, absent-minded professor look. His slight build, punctuated by a modestly overweight stomach, drew a sharp physical contrast with virtually all of the athletes who made up his students.

Cusac hesitantly addressed the class. "So, I'll introduce myself. I just retired from Duke, a little earlier than I thought I would.

I have moved to Shelby to help my niece, Donna, finish her life. She's dying from cancer. And I'm now to be the guardian of her intellectually disabled eleven-year-old. I've committed to a two-year contract here at Gardner-Webb, and you will have me for the rest of this semester, what's left of it." After a short pause and a sly smile, he added, "unless you run me away like you did the last teacher." As he spoke, most of the students sat up straight in their seats, showing respectful interest in his story and appreciating his quip. He finished telling them a bit more about who he was and why he had taken this job of teaching basic math concepts to athletes. He added, "And this will be a real class. I've been told that my contract hinges on some actual learning going on here."

Cusac paused, received no comments or questions from the class, and resumed speaking. "Now that you know a little about me, it's your turn. What's your interest in this math course, why are you taking it, what do you want to accomplish with it?" He looked back at the woman who commented about his briefcase, gestured with an open hand and said, "You first, go."

"I'm here to get this math credit. I need it to stay on the team," she replied in a matter of fact way. The other members of the class in turn described their own version of a need to get a math requirement out of the way and keep their athletic eligibility in place, but a small, thin boy named Miles added more. "Well, same for me. I'm a distance runner, but frankly, what I would love is to have you teach me something about statistics so I could win the Billion Dollar Bracket." The class laughed, some of them groaned sarcastically.

Cusac's disappointment had grown as each student identified his class as little more than a hurdle to jump. He asked himself if he might find just one motivated, challenging student who wanted to change the world with mathematics. He welcomed Miles's remark as the only reply that gave him some hope.

"Tell me about this . . . what . . . $1B you hope to win?" he asked.

Miles replied, "Well, if you know anything about basketball, you know there's a tournament going on, and this year we are in it!" The class erupted with applause. Three students leaned over to one very tall, blond young man seated in the middle of the group and slapped him repeatedly on the back. The recipient of the attention smiled broadly and gave a subdued fake-bow while remaining seated, his large hands wrapped around the front of the desk. Two other students turned to a smaller African-American student seated in the back and exchanged hand slaps and fist bumps. Cusac joined in with measured applause, hoping that he had managed to obscure the fact he had no clue about what they were talking about.

Miles jumped back in to the conversation and, with help from others in the class, described the Las Vegas-based contest to pick a perfect bracket and, in doing so, win $1B. Feeling a seed of hope that he might have found a way to engage the students, Cusac surprised the class with what he said next. "So, if I understand the concept of this bracket, it's about predicting the outcome of basketball games. How about if we use this basketball bracket thing as a way to get into some math?"

Miles broke the silence. "You mean do this in class? How's that going to work?"

"Well, you tell me. Do you think that making predictions might have something to do with numbers and statistics? Could be some mathematical constructions involved here. I dare to think that Las Vegas odds-makers might be kind of interested in math." Cusac got no reply, but he could see some growing interest on the faces of the students.

"So, it would be sort of a class project?" one student asked.

"A project or maybe even the whole structure of the class. How long does this tournament go on? Even if the tournament ends before the end of the semester, we'd still have a lot of data to review and maybe, I guess, try to see what we did right and did wrong. When is this tournament, anyway?"

"Well, it actually starts tomorrow, but the Billion Dollar Bracket Contest gives you a pass on the play-in games, so you don't really have to send in your picks until eight a.m. on Thursday."

"I'm sure someone will tell me what 'getting a pass on play-in games' is in reference to. Maybe I can learn something too. But it sounds like if we want to do this, we need to get busy. We have this class and Wednesday to get something done."

Another student chimed in. "Oh, we can pick a bracket right now."

Cusac interrupted. "I'm sure you can, but that's not the point. The point is learning some math as you do it. Are you in or not?"

"Sure, but you'll have to tell us where we're going with this math thing, Professor Cusac."

Pleased that he had just been addressed with a title of respect, Cusac took the lead. "Okay, here we go. Let's start with a basic concept. Does anyone here know the definition of a formula?"

Blank stares dominated until a female student spoke up, clearly reading from her cell phone. "A formula is a mathematical relationship or rule expressed by symbols."

"Correct, Miss . . . what is your name?"

"Rebecca."

"Correct, Rebecca. You get a point for class participation, but going forward I want you to use your noodle and not your Google. Understand?" She quickly put her phone down on her desk and covered it with a notebook in a playful mockery of hiding the offending device.

"So, yes, a formula is a mathematical rule, law, or relationship expressed in symbols, usually including letters of the alphabet with which you are familiar, and sometimes using symbols that are more obscure, depending on the understanding of what the symbol represents. But let's keep it simple for now. Can anyone give me an example of a formula?"

No one spoke, so Cusac elaborated. "I'll help you out, using letters of the alphabet, the letter *a* plus the letter *b* equals the letter *c*. Simply put, if you add what *a* represents to what *b* represents, you get *c*. Now I want you put on your thinking cap and tell me something that might fit into this formula."

Rebecca cautiously offered an answer. "So, if you have *a* represent ice and have *b* represent water, then *c* would be ice water?"

The class howled with what most thought was a silly reply, but Cusac interrupted loudly,

"No, don't laugh. That's exactly right. She got the point exactly right. The letters stand in for something more complex. That's what a symbol is. And the whole point is to give you a simple and universal language."

"Like a recipe?" asked another student from the back of the room.

"Yes, that's in the right direction, generally speaking, but we want to make it specific to math, moving beyond eggs plus milk plus cheese equals quiche."

The class laughed again but then grew quiet. Most were clearly engaged in the discussion. Cusac pushed forward. "So, now let's make it relevant to what we want to do to win $1B. What if we say, for a specific basketball game, that the letter *c* represents a win, or rather the expectation that a team would win the game. Then you tell me what would *a* and *b* represent in order to equal a win. And it has to be something you can measure, not just something like hard work or good luck."

A voice called out from the back of the class. "You mean like a won-loss record?"

"Great. What else?"

"Maybe the average point spread?" Miles put in, then seeing

Cusac did not understand the term he added, "That's the average number of points a team scores versus the number of points a team allows?"

"Now we're getting somewhere. Even I can see that could have predictive value."

Miles raised his hand and spoke. "I'm a little confused. You can't put numbers down for a team without comparing it to the team they are playing."

Cusac's excitement grew with Miles's grasp of the issue, but he cautioned, "Slow down. We'll get there. Little steps for little feet. Right now, I'm simply interested in coming up with some things we can measure that might be relevant to a team's opportunity to win an athletic contest. But we have our starting point. Anyone here know where I'm going next?"

Rebecca answered, "Many, many things can be measured, like won-loss and scoring differentials. You could drive yourself crazy with what kinds of obscure statistics you can find on the Internet, or what the sports announcers talk about every day."

Cusac opened his arms wide, lifted his gaze to the ceiling, and spoke with a faux dramatic tone. "Rebecca just gave you, class, your assignment. Between now and Wednesday's class, your assignment is to get creative and identify as many things as you can that you think would be important to indicate that a team might be worthy of success, or not worthy. But something to measure. To *measure*. That's the key. All science follows from measurement. Whether it's about the stars in the nighttime sky or the level of sugar in the blood, it's about numbers and what you can or can *not* measure."

Cusac then pulled himself back from his short reverie, aware he was approaching the self-indulgent place to which he sometimes traveled when standing before an audience of students. He concluded the class with a few clarifications. "We will meet on Wednesday, and I will add another concept to the one of 'formula.'

If you wish, you may look it up beforehand. It is the concept of 'equation', a companion and complementary concept to what we have introduced today."

"Then we will fill out a bracket?" Miles asked.

"Yes, I guess. Let me think about how to divide this up in order to be efficient, if our deadline is Thursday morning. Can someone tell me how many teams are in the tournament?"

"Sixty-four. Divided into four separate regions. If you don't count the play-in games. If you do, then there's sixty-eight."

"Okay. There are those pesky play-in games again. But . . . sixty-four divided by four is sixteen, and we have seventeen students in this class. Sixteen plus one. Hmmm . . . let me think about this."

Miles raised and waved his hand excitedly. "We could assign four students to each region, and I'll volunteer to be a wild card and help all of them out."

The class jeered at Miles. "Going for the extra credit right off the bat, eh, Miles?" added the student to his left.

Cusac cut the jeers short. "That's actually a good idea, Miles. Four groups of four will each take a . . . I think you called it a 'region,' and each group will submit a bracket for class study and discussion. Then Miles will submit his own, and I will prepare another. We will submit my bracket to the actual contest, just for fun. And if I win, I will keep the $1B, and you get something far more valuable: the ability to understand mathematical concepts. Class dismissed."

The class laughed and groaned at Cusac's comment about the relative value of $1B versus mathematical understanding, but smiles filled the room. Most students filed out promptly, but Rebecca and Miles came to the front of the room to ask more questions. Cusac felt a sense of relief and encouragement that at least he had two engaged students. He made a mental note to investigate the odds of picking all the winners in a tournament of sixty-four or sixty-eight teams. Then he chuckled at himself for thinking: *Just maybe . . .*

4

CHEEKY

His classes over for the day, Cusac drove several miles to the campus of Crest High School, the location of an after-school program for special-needs students. Greeted at the door by Davita Thompson, a tall, thin black woman who was the administrator and lead teacher of the program, he soon found himself seated at a table on one side of a large classroom. From across the room he observed his eleven-year-old grandniece, who everyone called "Cheeky," working with an older student tutor. The tutor and Cheeky sat with backs turned toward the others and did not appear to note their presence.

Ms. Thompson spoke in a quiet voice as they watched tutor and student work through an assignment. "Cheeky's strengths are verbal. She's working on vocabulary. She has a particular affinity for words that rhyme. We're using that interest to help her build on what she knows and needs to know. Let's listen for a minute."

"A bear has hair," the tutor spoke, smiling at Cheeky, and then paused, expecting a reply.

Cheeky laughed and repeated the words "bear" and "hair." She slowly added, "I know bear. I know hair."

As Cusac watched, he reflected on the fact that Cheeky did not appear obviously mentally deficient or disabled. She had a ready smile and looked healthy and fit. Cusac posed a question that he knew about generally but wanted to hear more. "So, where does she test now as far as age level?"

Ms. Thompson opened a file and ran her finger over some test results as she explained, "Overall, when you look at her capabilities, she has a grasp of information and performs pretty much at kindergarten or first-grade level. But it's more complicated than that. We're optimistic. We think she can learn far above that."

"That's a little vague. What's her IQ?" Cusac asked with a puzzled look on his face.

"I don't actually have that in front of me, and frankly in this program it's not that useful. For kids like Cheeky, it's not a number that you want to base your expectations on. She has such a range of capabilities. Very low in math. Much better in verbal. She has these little discrete areas that make you call her 'smart' in some ways."

Cusac interrupted, showing impatience, "Well, I feel like I need something more tangible if I'm going to be her, uh, caretaker. Can you give me something more specific?"

Ms. Thompson answered patiently, "She's not really intellectually disabled in the way most people think about it. She shows a very inconsistent set of talents. But the really good thing about Cheeky is that if you spend any time around her, you can pretty much see she was really loved and taken care of. She loves and trusts people. Might not be totally prepared for the rough and tumble of middle school right around the corner, but she has a good emotional foundation if her situation is managed well. I think you should find her a very rewarding child."

Cusac looked down at the table. "So, is she autistic?"

"That's another one of those labels that seem to me to be changing and evolving all the time. I'd steer clear of putting any label of expectation on her in planning for her future. Like I said, she's a really great kid to work with, and I love working with her."

Cusac received Ms. Thompson's reply with a combination of

hope and concern. His mind filled with unanswerable questions about what he would be called upon to do, to guide her to maturity, and what the future ultimately held for her.

"So, how well does Cheeky know you?" Ms. Thompson asked.

"I've spent a few hours in the past with her and her mother, but never alone with Cheeky one-on-one. And now I've been in their guest room for three days. We're trying to work out what to do with living arrangements. I'm renting an apartment for the short term. But to answer your question, Cheeky knows me a little and seems to be comfortable with me. I have a lot of work to do in order to do this."

"So, just how did you become the one to take care of Cheeky after her mother is no longer around?" Cusac felt something akin to disapproval in her question, and grew silent.

Ms. Thompson saw his reaction and responded, "I'm sorry. That sounded a bit nosy, and it's really not any of my business."

"No. That's fine. A fair question from someone who I can see cares about her. It's a long story. I'll give you the short version. First, there was no one else to do this. It was me or foster care or an institution."

Ms. Thomson smiled approvingly and Cusac continued. "As for me, personally, why I made the decision to step up, well, let's just say I have an ex-wife who barely speaks to me and two children who will take a phone call from me, but not much talking goes on when they do. I was a lot better math teacher than I was a father and husband. When the kids were grown, the three of them, counting their mother, pretty much left me. I didn't actually do anything bad, I think. I just didn't do anything good with them, really. I'm not important to them. I guess they felt they were not important to me. I don't have a clue about how to make it any better. Maybe now, here—"

Devita Thompson interrupted. "I didn't mean to—"

"No. It's really okay," Cusac continued quickly. "None of this is a secret. And now I have a dead sister, and her daughter, Donna, is dying, and Cheeky really has nobody else in a position to help. So, why am I the one to help Cheeky? Boil it down to my opportunity to prove I can be important to someone."

After a brief silence signified both were satisfied that was enough information for now, Ms. Thompson offered to do what she could to help, and their conversation turned back to Cheeky. The tutorial session soon ended. Cusac and Ms. Thompson stood to greet the others. Cheeky walked directly to Cusac and gave him a hug, placing the side of her head on his upper arm. "Ready to go home and see Mom?" he asked. Cheeky nodded but looked sad. Cusac noticed her downcast face but couldn't find the words to ask about it.

After a short drive to Cheeky's and her mother's home, Cusac rang the front doorbell, then knocked on the door, but Donna did not answer. As Cusac did not yet have a key to the house, he and Cheeky spent a few worrisome moments trying to decide what to do. Cusac thought Cheeky was going to cry. He posed a question, partly to Cheeky, but mostly out loud to himself, "I wonder if there's a key hidden around here somewhere outside?"

Cheeky's face lit up. "I know where the key is." She went directly to a small flowerpot and took the key from underneath it.

"That's my girl," Cusac beamed and reached to take the key, but she rushed past him and quickly moved to the door. Her fingers trembled and, for a moment, she seemed upset but soon successfully opened the door and rushed in.

Once inside, they found Donna sleeping soundly. Cusac felt profoundly uncomfortable approaching her, having little experience with illness and death. Her breathing seemed normal, but there was a bottle of medication on the floor beside her bed. Contrary to his first fear that she might have taken an overdose, Cusac was relieved to find the bottle was almost full. He reluctantly turned his attention to waking her up. With Cheeky standing beside him, he put his hand on her shoulder and called her name.

She moaned, then awakened, startled. "What . . . who . . . huh . . . I'm awake . . . I'm getting up." Cheeky turned and left the room, clearly upset. Donna struggled beneath the covers, trying to rise, then fell back into the bed.

Cusac addressed her again. "Donna, just relax. I was going to leave, but I can stay and help with dinner. Would that be helpful?"

Donna blinked and then rubbed her eyes, pulling the covers tightly around her neck as she spoke. "Yeah . . . well . . . weren't you going to work on your apartment? But okay, if you can stay." She drifted back to sleep for another half hour while Cheeky and Cusac prepared soup and noodles.

Later, during the meal, Donna remained groggy and confused, apologizing twice and explaining that she must have taken too much pain medicine. Unprompted, she added, "When I'm gone, I know you will do everything you can, and I know Cheeky will be okay." She spoke bluntly, with little expression and no eye contact with either of the others.

"Where are you going, Mommy?" Cheeky asked. Cusac felt lost in knowing how to join or whether to redirect the conversation. He had anticipated some planning for this discussion, at least the part that included Cheeky.

"I'm going to die, girl. You know . . . you know about people dying. Like your grandfather." Cheeky's mother said this as she reached for a glass of water and clumsily tipped it, catching it just before it spilled over. "At least I'm not going to leave on purpose like your father. I don't want to leave. I don't want to die." Donna put her fork down on her plate, leaving most of the food untouched. She sat lost in her own thoughts, unaware of how her daughter might be affected by her words. Her face betrayed changing expressions, from sadness to anger. Cusac grew fearful about what she might say next.

Cheeky looked confused and anxious. One moment tearful, then quiet and motionless, staring at her food, but she did not move from the table. Cusac intervened and gently but promptly led Donna away and back to her bedroom. She did not resist, and fell asleep immediately after being tucked into bed. Cusac picked up the bottle of pain pills and put them in his pocket.

When he returned to the kitchen, he knew he needed to help Cheeky understand more. He asked, "Cheeky, what have people told you about your mother being sick?" Cheeky looked anxious and tears formed in the corners of her eyes. She tried to speak several times but stopped short of giving any real answer.

He tried again. "I think your mother said something about your grandfather. Is that right?" Cheeky became stone-faced and would not make eye contact.

Cusac realized he was not helping her. They both welcomed a change of topic to refocus on the food they were eating.

Late that night, after all were settled and in bed, Cusac lay awake realizing how little he knew about Cheeky's family. He didn't know the story of how and why her father left them. He did know there was no financial support from the father, no personal contact, only some attorney fees having to do with court battles not yet over. He became acutely aware that he knew nothing about how to help children—or adults for that matter—talk about death. He wondered if Davita Thompson's offer of help would include something that could help him with this. He questioned the wisdom of his willingness to take on this role. The decision now seemed impulsive, maybe even foolishly idealistic, and certainly not consistent with the well-planned and cautious way he had always lived his life.

STUDENT TEACHES
THE TEACHER

The next day, Lewis Cusac sat beside Miles, his most enthusiastic student, in a booth of the Snack Shop just across
the street from the Gardner-Webb campus. Cusac scanned
pictures hanging on the bright-red and black inside walls of the
restaurant, commenting, "Well, it looks like about a hundred years
of history of the school, especially the sports teams, right there on
the walls. Don't have to guess what the school colors are. Do you
know these pictures?"

"I know a lot of them," said Miles. "But the owner is kind of a
godfather to some of the teams. He can talk your head off all day
long if you have the time and are brave enough to actually ask him
a question."

Cusac shook his head, indicating he would pass on that level of
interest.

Miles continued, "See the team picture up at the top? The one
pretty much yellowed out? The one on the end in street clothes is
my grandfather. He was sort of an all-purpose student manager of
the basketball team in the mid to late sixties." Miles explained that
his father and grandfather both had earned degrees at Gardner-
Webb before him and that when Miles was a child, his family lived
within walking distance of the campus.

Students filed in and out of the busy Snack Shop on their way to early classes, carrying take-out cups of coffee and pastries, moving cautiously around each other in the narrow space between the booths and the line of circular stools at the long counter, oblivious to Miles and Cusac.

"Maybe someday I'll ask about some of the pictures, but not today. We need to focus on our brackets," Cusac answered, shuffling several pieces of paper he had printed from the Internet contest to assist in picking the winners of the NCAA Basketball Tournament.

Miles moved his laptop a few inches closer to his companion and pointed out a website that presented an inexhaustible display of information about all the teams playing in the tournament.

"So, if you don't wanna just go with your instincts or first impressions, and you're really serious about trying to come up with a useful 'formula,' here's stuff you could study for hours. We've got mind-numbing numbers, but it's measurable." Miles pointed at the screen. "And if you want to listen to the self-appointed experts about who's going to spring an upset, go to that site there, or just glue yourself to ESPN for the next two days."

Cusac raised an eyebrow. "By 'upset,' I assume you mean when a team is not favored to win, but somehow does? How often does that happen? Do we have statistics on that?"

Cusac saw that Miles looked puzzled and asked, "What? Am I asking dumb questions? You know that the only really dumb question is the one that you don't ask. So, bear with me here; I admit it, when it comes to basketball, I don't know a lot."

"I gotcha, Doc, here we go." Miles then launched into educating his instructor with an energetic description of the unpredictability of any specific game between any two teams. "It's like there is some sort of magic when a team that should lose by twenty points somehow gets it goin' and plays way above their heads. Or the other way around, a team that has played great all year ends up flat on a particular night and stinks out the gym. That's the beauty of it if you win, and the heartbreak if you're the loser."

Cusac frowned. "So, how many variables are we dealing with here? Can we put them in categories?"

"You mean things as simple as won-lost records, or how they did if they already played each other this year? Actually, look at the bracket. Most of the obvious stuff is already counted in the seeding they get." Sounding to Cusac like a sportscaster on an early morning talk show, Miles went on to describe how the bracket committee determined if a certain team would get a seeding with a low number, which meant they performed better during the year so far, and should generally be favored against a team with a higher number. Miles offered one anecdote after another about what teams accomplished to deserve a higher rank than some other team.

Cusac noticed Miles's energy and enthusiasm for tournament trivia. He allowed himself to hope that kind of energy could carry over to basic math concepts for the students in his class.

"So, what would be wrong with just picking the team with the higher seed, uh, the lower number?"

Cusac noticed a momentary eye roll in Miles's expression but ignored it, accepting that he deserved it for his inexperience with the fortunes of college basketball. Miles continued, "Because you'd get about a fourth of them wrong. There are always upsets. And for two teams, one with a number eight and the other a number nine seed, there isn't really much of a favorite. They are pretty much even."

Cusac held up both palms, as if apologizing for another naive question. "So, let me get this straight here. All the teams in the tournament are matched up in the first games by having the best teams play the lesser teams?"

"Right. They are, as we said in class, divided into four regions. In each region, the highest rated is a one and the lowest a sixteen."

"And how often does a sixteen-seeded team beat a number one?"

"It's only happened once, and that's depressing." Miles grimaced.

"Why is it depressing?"

"Because we are in the tournament and we're ranked as a sixteen, and that means we are playing a one."

"Do fifteens ever beat twos?" Cusac asked.

"Yeah, that happens from time to time. Not every year, and it's always a story—"

Cusac interrupted. "I can't imagine there's that much difference between teams rated ones or twos and between teams rated sixteen or fifteen."

Miles responded with increased enthusiasm. "Okay, I think I see where you may be going here, the emotional factor. Does a team actually believe they can win? And at some point, the numbers have a little voodoo in them. When you get down to a twelve playing a five, that's where you start to see the upsets. Seems to happen every year. Twelves beat fives all the time. Happens more often than an eleven beating a six. Tell me how that makes sense."

"What were you saying about the emotional factor? I don't really know what to do with that," Cusac said.

Miles pushed the laptop away and settled back into his seat. His face showed uncertainty about how to proceed with Cusac's education about the world of college basketball. Cusac saw Miles withdraw and felt embarrassed at his lack of understanding about the sport.

"Don't give up on me Miles. I'm at least aware of how little I know."

Miles took a deep breath and continued. "You have to understand that every team has their own story, their own tradition. And certain matchups, like when Michigan plays Michigan State, or Kentucky plays Louisville, it gets really personal. Think of games like that as bragging rights for the state, but it goes even deeper. And don't get me started about Duke and Carolina. It's like class warfare."

"I understand that. I was at Duke. I saw the emotional irrationality. More than once, I had to step over students in sleeping bags who were camped out to get tickets to a game. I just don't know how to operationalize it. I suppose the emotion that influences motivation is a legitimate key statistical variable. Hard to measure, but there must be ways to think about it. It's probably what the Las Vegas odds makers do all the time. I want to look at those websites and look for other variables, but first tell me about Gardner-Webb being in the tournament. I don't want to seem stupid in front of the class. What's the story you talk about? What's the local tradition that might have something to do with this game?"

Miles's eyes brightened. "Well, now that you mention it, there is a story here. We are playing Kentucky, the number one team in the East Regional, and we actually did beat them once back in 2007."

"Gardner-Webb beat Kentucky?"

"Yeah, shows up on all the top ten lists of greatest upsets ever in any sport. Right up there with Appalachian beating Michigan in football and the U.S. beating Russia in hockey."

"So, why is it impossible to think it couldn't happen again?"

"Payback. Most people think this game will be motivation for a real slaughter by Kentucky. It'll probably be a big revenge story, kind of like *The Empire Strikes Back*, if you get my drift. We'll get a thrashing for humiliating them last time. Even the ESPN announcers were talking the other day about how it was just plain wicked for the tournament selection committee to pair us up with them. A real setup for a beatdown of legendary proportions."

"So, how many people in the Billion Dollar Bracket contest will pick Gardner-Webb to win?"

"Uh, like, zero."

Cusac smiled and stretched. He pulled Miles's laptop over to his seat and clicked through the website that Miles had recommended. "This is actually going to be fun. See, here's the strategy. We look at all the obvious outcomes, the sixteens versus the ones, even the fifteens and twos, but then we drill down on the individual stories. I'm looking here at this web site, and just by scanning titles of stories, I can see some obvious variables."

Miles joined Cusac in surveying the data. "What jumps out at you?"

"I see a story about this one team that's got all seniors on it playing another that has almost all first-year players, freshmen, except one sophomore."

"Yeah, but the thing is that not a single one of those seniors are a lock to be drafted by the NBA, but all those first-year stars will be first- or second-round Pro Picks at the end of the year or the next. One or two of them might decide to stay another year if they think it translates to a higher number in the draft pick, meaning a bigger shoe contract. Just a lot more talented than the older guys."

Cusac frowned. "Shoe contract. Okay, I guess I get that, the Nike thing. But what you're really pointing out is that some guys a year out of high school, eighteen and nineteen years old, are better than guys with four years of experience and three years older?"

Miles smiled. "That's the way it is. So, now you tell me how math and statistics can help sort that kind of thing out."

Cusac gave Miles no reply but continued to scroll through the computer's offerings. He mumbled half-completed thoughts about what he saw on the screen including injury reports, shared opponents, matchups between coaches, and more. After five minutes of his reverie, all the while ignoring Miles, Cusac snapped the computer shut and smiled. "This is going to be so much fun. Buckle your seat belts for the classroom. I'm takin' you folks for a ride. When did you say the bracket needs to be filled out? By Thursday, early in the day?"

"Right, eight a.m., just a few hours before the first game starts," replied Miles. "One more thing, along the lines of you not feeling stupid there in the class, just so you know, two of the team's best players are in the class. Did you notice the tall blond guy in the middle of the room?"

"The one everybody was slapping on the back?" Cusac asked.

"That's the one. He's Simon Bradley, freshman superstar from Australia. He's likely— no, he's a lock to go pro after this year. He's 90 percent of why we made the tournament. No, actually, he's more like 99 percent of why we won our conference tournament. The other player is the stocky black guy in the back, Roma Hill, a senior from New York City. The two of them are *the* dynamic duo on the court, and they're inseparable off the court. It's the worst kept secret in the world that Roma was assigned by the coaches to be Simon's big brother, keep him focused on basketball, out of trouble, and keep him hittin' the books to stay eligible."

"Hey, that's a story all by itself. Young, vulnerable guy half a world away from home, under pressures he never imagined, mentored by a savvy street kid."

"Something like that." Miles responded mechanically and looked away as he gathered up his computer and papers. Cusac felt that Miles's last comment held unspoken meaning, but did not follow up on his curiosity. Cusac's thoughts were elsewhere, dancing with statistics, formulas, and a new sort of playing field on which to layer mathematical concepts. By now he knew the odds against perfection, but . . . *hey, a boy can dream.*

BRACKET ENTRIES—
THE MADNESS BEGINS

Back in Sinclair Dane's conference room, now transformed over the last six weeks into what she called her "war room," a half-dozen desktop and an equal number of laptop computers framed the conference room table. Two or three people jockeyed for space around each monitor. Several others sat in chairs away from the table, using smaller handheld devices including cell phones. Stacks of magazines, newspapers, and various books filled the center of the table.

On one wall a long, printed banner read "WE ARE NOW THE CONSORTIUM." Multiple hand-lettered signs reminded all that today was Tuesday, two days before the first games. Colorful "action station" signs in three corners of the room identified Social Media, Advertising, and Bracket Entry areas. Several people moved purposefully from group to group, collecting information and passing it on to others.

Sinclair, Rod Browning, and Marilyn Seale stood in the hall looking through the open conference room door, speaking softly, discussing the staff the three partners had put together. For the advertising component, Rod had hired four recent graduates of an advertising degree program at a school where he regularly taught some of the real-world aspects of the marketing and advertising business. Those four were charged with brainstorming how ads should look and how to convince other companies to buy advertising on the Billion Dollar Bracket website.

Rod spoke. "So far, we have rough designs for apparel, beer and soft drinks, sports gear, and so on. We've made a hundred hours of cold calls to potential buyers." Rod paused, glancing at Marilyn. "We have more than two dozen companies who are considering signing on but only one taker so far. Want to hear about that one?"

"In a minute," interrupted Sinclair. "But first I want to hear about the others in the room, the social media team. Marilyn?"

"Well, as you can see, it's a young group. That's who we could get to work in limited time positions on short notice with the job description you gave me. None of them have regular jobs but seem to make a living freelancing this and that, focused on social media. But it's a smart group. We can go in and talk to Lilith if you want to. She's the team leader. She's busy, but she can stop what she's doing if you want to meet her."

"How many on her team?"

"Eight more, in addition to her, and a few more coming. She's the one right in the middle of the left side of the table. The one with all the metal piercings and tattoos." Marilyn had pointed out a thin, pale-skinned twenty-something woman in a T-shirt and jeans, her left arm tattooed with a colorful sea scene featuring fish, sailing ships, and seashells. Her ears and nose were pierced and laden with gold and silver adornments.

"How did the team-building go?" Sinclair asked.

"It didn't. We gave up on it less than an hour in."

Sinclair shot back, "I thought we agreed that—"

"I know what we discussed. And I'm not saying your experience with that kind of group bonding stuff that you used to do isn't worthwhile, but when we got this group together, the only people who paid attention to me were the IT guys." Marilyn gestured toward two clean-cut young men all typing at lightning speed into their computers. "And to some extent Rod's advertising team. But Lilith and her crew kept texting, dozing, or just generally zoning out. By the time we got through introductions, it was clear no one wanted to do the touchy-feely-groupie stuff, so we just talked about the project. But they were actually pretty sharp and enthusiastic about what they were being hired to do, once it was clearly laid out. Some of these kids have skills I don't. It's kind of anxiety-producing to be supervising people who are smarter than you are, but that's what we've got. And they kept saying they wanted to get to it, so we rebooted, so to speak, and jumped right in."

Sinclair frowned. "I just don't like the way this is starting."

Marilyn smiled back at her. "Step inside and listen. I think you'll like it a little more than you seem to." The three moved just inside the room, positioning themselves against the wall, out of the way of those working the computers. Competing noise from multiple conversations rose and fell as various forms of data became available for analysis and discussion.

A young man with orange hair shouted above the din, to whomever was listening and to no one in particular, "We just passed 30 million entries at two dollars each. That's thirty-six hours in. And get this; 16 percent are from China. 11 percent from Russia. Who the hell in China and Russia cares about this?"

A voice answered from another corner of the room, "Maybe the people who know about the Xavier point guard named Lavarov. He's goin' in the first round, NBA. He's a legend already in Russia! China has two freshmen twins that play for St. Johns. They're good, and they're good lookin'. Think deodorant commercials with no shirts."

Another voice shouted a question above the others, "Isn't there a guy from South Korea who's makin' a splash . . . where . . . Oklahoma State . . . you know, the seven-footer?"

"So, that's why we got a solid 6 percent from South Korea."

"And these are all paying the two dollars?" someone asked.

"All the online entries are paying; it's only the mailed-in paper ones that are free."

"How many of those do we have?"

A sarcastic voice gave the obvious reply, "Uh, maybe zero. The mail hasn't come yet."

"You won't believe who I got a bracket from," shouted another.

"Maybe Obama? When he was president, he always made a pick."

"Bigger. Bigger than Obama."

"Who's bigger than Obama? Oprah?"

"Bigger. We just got a bracket from the pope!" The room erupted in laughter and applause.

Sinclair Dane motioned her group back out into the hallway and took a wide-eyed deep breath. She started to ask a question, then stopped and changed the subject to another topic. "Lots to talk about here. Where to start? We need to regroup. No. This is good. This is *really* good. We've spent modestly on ads so far. It's almost all free social media, person to person. It's madness. March Madness! And with that number of entries, we may be looking at a possible perfect first-round bracket. I've been playing with this algorithm in my head about when entries might come in, and— ".

Rod Browning interrupted with a deep frown on his face. "A perfect first round? Would that mean we're in trouble?"

"Not at all. A perfect first round means either that somebody picked all the upsets, or that there were few or no upsets. You don't want upsets. Lots of upsets means a kind of predictability going forward. The teams that upset better teams will have to then play even better ones and probably won't do it twice. Few or no upsets means that most of the good teams are still in it and, in the next round, evenly matched. And harder to predict."

Rod saw that Sinclair was reassured by what she saw going on in the room. He welcomed her renewed enthusiasm. She continued, "The best analysis is that successful prediction is most difficult in the middle rounds. Now if someone's perfect up to the last eight or final four, then that is when we panic." Sinclair punched the word "panic" and added a smile and a wink.

Rod and Marilyn continued to have puzzled looks on their faces, so Sinclair continued. "No, I mean it. It's really . . . it's a good thing. A perfect first-round bracket means more attention, and more attention means advertising dollars coming to our website. Rod, that's why I've been pushing you to get those designs ready and make all those contacts. This is how we go from buying ads to selling ads."

Rod nodded enthusiastically. "Okay, now it's starting to come together. It makes sense if we have a perfect first-round bracket. Then eyes will be on us. Eyes will be on—"

Sinclair interrupted, "On the guy—or gal—with the perfect bracket and the congratulations coming in from Pepsi and Mountain Dew. Advertising dollars will flow from companies who want to associate with the genius with the perfect bracket, but it has to happen fast. We'll know about midnight on the first Friday of the tournament, meaning three days from now, if there is a perfect first round. And the ads will have to hit the airways by noon the next day. Bring your sleeping bag for a sleepover." Sinclair pumped her arms up and down with closed fists, smiling broadly at the others.

Rod answered sheepishly, "Okay. I'm not sure I truly understood all that. I think I've got some work to do. But I still haven't told you about the one advertising contract that we received. It's with a new start-up that is trying to compete with PayPal. We put an app on our website for entries to download and pay us through the new company. It's called *Ring-It*, and it's looking for a niche for small transactions. The way the contract is structured, we get the whole two dollars that comes with the entry fee, in return for a banner on our site, no transaction fee, and when we go over a certain amount, they pay us."

"Are they paying us yet?"

Rod shook his head as he answered, "Not yet, but if the numbers they're talking about in the room are right, and keep coming in as you project, they will buy some serious advertising from us before it's over. I did my research. They have the money. It's a good outfit. Sounds like 30 million people have already seen them and if we have a perfect first-round bracket, millions more will see their name. Even though entries are closed, people will flock to our website just to enjoy the chase for the $1B. I need to check how many people downloaded their app. If people download their app and actually use it for transactions beyond this entry transaction, we get paid for that."

Sinclair smiled but did not allow herself a happy dance just yet. "Listen, this part is gravy. I didn't expect the response we have. I'll be honest, being able to actually sell advertising is more than I had really hoped for. But think of it as the world we live in. The world is going crazy over a game that sneakers and workout gear makes glamorous. I'm sure both of you have a few pairs of hundred-dollar Nike shoes in your closet." Sinclair saw the puzzled looks on their faces and smiled. "You don't have to answer that."

Sinclair then turned to Marilyn. "I think I understand your work the least. Tell me how you did it so far. And how much have we spent on social media advertising?"

Marilyn replied after a deep breath. "Well, first, we've spent whatever we're paying the team to post on Facebook and Twitter, and a few others, all those social media opportunities that don't require an actual charge. You can do a lot of this for free. We did invest some from the initial investment of your money, but that has already been recovered."

"Really?" beamed Sinclair.

"Really. You've got those numbers about what we pay Lilith's team. It's not a lot. There isn't any other cost, except the five hundred we paid for the rights to use this YouTube of a guy doing trick shots from the far end of a basketball court. We'll show it to you when Joel gets it ready."

Sinclair smiled and nodded her approval, and Marilyn continued: "One surprising thing, but one that should not have been so hard to predict, is that the social media traffic has exploded in those countries that have foreign players on teams in the tournament. South Korea, China, and Russia have these young players who have become heroes in their own part of the world. It's a little scary, actually. The Russian guy already has a thousand online marriage offers from his own country. Australia is another, and it's the puzzle. But I still don't know about any player from Australia."

Sinclair pumped her fist in the air. "Good job! Go Facebook! Go Twitter! And all those other insta-face things! You have most likely increased your payday by something like five- to sixfold. More money for you, more money for all of us."

Both Rod and Marilyn stammered out words of disbelief. "What? How?"

"Do the numbers. I'll check my algorithm, but if entries come in at anything like the current rate for the next thirty-six hours, we realistically could approach gross income of $200M. We still have two more days for people to submit a bracket online. And that's without actually selling any advertising."

Sinclair smiled and, with mock dramatic fanfare, gestured with outstretched arms to re-direct attention to the conference room. The three of them stood silent, watching the cacophonous but controlled activity in the room. Staffers were laughing, pumping fists, and gulping down copious amounts of everything from Red Bull to Starbucks Doubleshot.

Sinclair turned back to her two partners, smiled, and said, "Game on."

Rod Browning and Marilyn Seale returned the smile, then realized how hard they would be working within the next two days and perhaps beyond. The first games were forty-eight hours away, but the tournament lasted three weeks. They left the office and walked outside to a warm March day. After brief goodbyes, Rod and Marilyn both ran to their cars to continue some of the work from their own offices. Rod turned back and shouted to Marilyn, "I got another idea! I just thought of another place we can sell this!"

Turning to go to her private office, Sinclair caught her foot on one of the dozen sleeping bags in the hallway and stumbled, but caught herself before she fell. She accepted the presence of the bags as a cluttered reminder that the plan was working. No one would be going home for the next few days, and money would keep flowing in. She tried to calculate in her head exactly how much, then gave up and broke into a big grin.

CUSAC'S BALANCING ACT

Cusac and Cheeky joined Miles, Roma Hill, and Simon Bradley on Tuesday evening seated around a table in the Snack Shop in Boiling Springs. The three student athletes had voiced their enthusiasm for meeting Cheeky once they'd learned the story of Cusac's relationship with her. Davida Thompson had encouraged Cusac to find ways to get Cheeky out of the house for social activities, away from the sadness of her mother's condition.

Feeling the pressure of having the students complete their assignments with only two remaining days before brackets were due, Cusac took a chance that Cheeky could tolerate some of the time with the men talking about the basketball tournament. Cusac relaxed when they all sat around the table together. Cheeky seemed to be having fun with attention from the three young men. He felt a sense of relief that he had made a good decision.

They shared an early evening dessert, and after some small talk about Cheeky, they turned their attention to basketball. Roma Hill took the lead for the discussion, enlivened by timely assistance from Miles. The group first discussed stories about odd and unexpected things that had happened in the NCAA tournament over the years. Key stories included such things as the death of a player's mother leading to the best single game he'd ever played. Another true legend covered how a broken leg suffered by the star of one team inspired his teammates to play far above expectations and come back from a large deficit to win a game that seemed at one point to be lost.

Sensitive to the fact that Cheeky had become quiet and now seemed restless, Roma Hill turned a smiling face to her. "So, people call you Cheeky. I love your name. I've just got to know how you got it."

Cheeky blushed and covered her face, but a big smile showed through the space between her hands. She let out an audible giggle. Cusac gave the answer. "Well, Cheeky, let me see if I have this right. Your mother said that from the time you could talk you had a great sense of humor, that you liked to laugh at funny words. Some words made you really laugh, and sometimes you would say really funny things when no one was expecting it. Do I have that right?"

Cheeky clearly enjoyed the attention from the group, but all she said was, "I dunno . . ."

The three students glanced around at each other, smiling at the girl. Cusac continued, "Okay, Cheeky, if you're not going to talk, I'm going to tell the story that your mother told me. Okay?"

Cheeky's smile gave consent, but all she said was "I dunn-oooooooo . . ." stretching out the last word in a way that made the others laugh.

Cusac continued, "Here's the story, as Cheeky's mother told it to me. A couple of years ago, two of Cheeky's classmates were having a fuss in the hallway between classes. A teacher was trying to break it up without much success. Cheeky sized up the situation and walked up to the two students and put first one hand on one girl's shoulder, then the other hand on the second student's shoulder and said, 'Breathe in . . . breathe out . . . breathe in . . . breathe out . . . take a little time. It's gonna be okay.'" As the three young men around the table burst into laughter, Cusac explained that a teacher then said, "Well, aren't you a cheeky little one."

Cusac added that Cheeky liked the sound of the word and took it as her name. Even though she didn't know what it really meant at first, she accepted that it meant somebody who says funny things.

As the story of Cheeky's name concluded, the group grew silent until Miles picked up a printout of some team statistics. Before he could speak, Cheeky interrupted him. She pointed across the table to Simon Bradley, who, like Cheeky, had been mostly quiet during the discussion at the table, and blurted out, "I give you a new name. You now Rhymin' Simon." Cheeky then laughed loudly, bouncing up and down in her seat, continuing to point at Simon Bradley.

Simon returned the laughter and the others joined in, laughing both at Cheeky's name for Simon and at the way Cheeky laughed at the name she had created for him.

After the laughter again died down, the group reviewed some statistics from previous tournaments. They focused on stories about teams losing players to injury late in the year. Miles had a list of recent injuries for key players. Cusac shook his head, expressing his doubt about trying to quantify this as a useful variable. Miles came back that the common wisdom was that for a game or two after losing a key player to injury, teams seem to pull together and play well without the player who was lost. He added that eventually the loss caught up to the team. Miles admitted this was anecdotal.

Roma then looked at his watch and exclaimed, "We're out of time, sorry, we've got to get back to the dorm for curfew. We leave tomorrow morning. Game's on Friday."

While Cusac understood, he frowned and added, "There's so much left to do. Guess we'll carry on without you two."

Cusac reached to pick up the check. Roma snapped it out of his hand saying, "No sir, under no circumstances will you be buying anything for us. The 'watchers' could be anywhere."

The puzzled look on Cusac's face required a detailed explanation. Miles took the lead.

"The NCAA could make something illegal out of even a dessert, and the players could end up in trouble with eligibility. Big trouble for the school too, even if it was just cheesecake."

Roma then collected the appropriate amounts of cash from everyone and paid at the counter on the way out. Miles and Cusac continued the discussion about the class for a few minutes more. On the way home, a happy Cheeky giggled and rhymed, "Rhymin' Simon! Rhymin' Simon. I like you, Rhymin' Simon!"

Cusac met with Miles over coffee before class the next morning to finish the planning that had taken place the night before. Cusac explained that he had felt surprised and curious about the fuss over the issue of his paying the cost of a dessert. He asked Miles about it again. "I can't believe I can't buy those guys a cheesecake."

"Yeah, and if you read the rulebook about what you can't do and what they can't do, it would make you crazy."

"Explain," said Cusac.

"I'll be happy to, Dr. Cusac, but first I just have to marvel a little at the fact that you, being a professor at Duke University, know so little about the world of college sports and money."

"Money?" Cusac replied in a straightforward way, showing he was beyond being embarrassed about what he did not know.

Miles raised his eyebrows and widened his eyes dramatically, adding an open palms-up gesture. "Yes, it's all about money, the money that flows from big television contracts to the schools and the NCAA for the labors of its students, or should I say the slave labor."

Miles and Cusac had, by this time, developed a capacity for some comfort with each other, but from the point that Miles used the term "slave labor," the conversation took an edgier tone.

"That's a pretty strong judgement you're passing there. Slave labor? What about the scholarship for the education they get?"

Miles came back quickly with a well-prepared answer. "Well, there's two things. First, far too many of the players who generate the excitement and the money—for the school—never get any kind of education. They get steered into crap classes, and even then, they don't actually get a degree."

Miles took a deep breath, slowing his answer, indicating this was a topic that held emotion for him. "Second, even for the ones that do, if you're a poor black or even a poor white kid, the limitations on what support you get means you attend school livin' in poverty. You don't have the money for the kind of clothes, spending money, and even all the educational supplies you need to succeed in being a real part of the big athlete's culture. Not too long ago, there was even a rule about how much they could spend on feeding athletes, and the kids that didn't have mommy and daddy sending money for late-night runs for cheeseburgers went to bed hungry. The food thing is a little better now."

Cusac frowned and continued with the questions: "And that's why someone like me can't help out? Even with a piece of cheesecake?"

Miles shot back, "You'd be amazed by the things you can't help out with. You can't help out by doing things like if a kid's grandmother who raised him dies mid-semester, and he has no way to get back home to Alabama from Ohio State, or if he falls down in the dorm and breaks his front teeth out, and he has no way to pay a dentist . . . and then if you pay for a trip home or a visit to a private dentist, he's ineligible and the school goes on NCAA probation." Miles punched the air with a finger as he made this point. His face reddened as he spat out the last few words.

Cusac could see Miles was angry about the issues discussed, and felt some need to tone things down, but he wanted to know more. "I'm grasping for a logical explanation for why things are this way."

"It's the whole student-athlete myth. It's not entirely a myth, but in the money-making sports of football and basketball, it's just a total scam that we're supposed to see these fantastic athletes as students first and—oh, by the way, they play football in their spare time. Most of 'em are there to bring in money for the school by entertaining the alumni and the rest of the world with big wins—and only wins matter—and their only payoff would be if they do sign a professional contract. Want to tell me what fraction of 1 percent actually do that?"

Cusac felt timid about his next question. "Has anyone ever considered a different track to the professional sports teams, maybe some kind of minor leagues? Like they do in baseball. I do know about that."

"Well, actually those things do exist. Basketball has developmental leagues and football has arena football, but neither that nor anything like it would ever be the glorious entertainment product that college football and basketball gives you. Too many pigs feeding from the bucket. College presidents, the NCAA, the television sports contracts. You do know what the first letter in ESPN stands for, don't you? It stands for 'entertainment.'"

Cusac continued to ask questions about this world he never knew about, and Miles needed little encouragement to continue. "It's a lot about loyalty and identity and how some people seem to make their college connection a central part of the rest of their lives. And then the money flows. And part of the money builds a recruiting machine, at least for the bigger schools, like Kentucky and Duke and UNC and all those. The recruiting machine gets into kids' lives really young. Really young. Even middle school. Some kids are so obviously talented by age twelve that they already have scouts coming to middle school basketball games."

Cusac smiled. "Gettin' yourself a little worked up here, are you Miles?"

Miles calmed himself with a pause and a deep breath, then

added, "And I say all of this knowing that without my 55 percent track scholarship I'd be in the military or working some crappy job and my Marine Corps father not speaking to me."

Cusac picked up the conversation without pause. "So, here's another question. How do the kids—the student athletes—learn or know the rules?"

His adrenaline apparently spent, Miles answered reflectively. "Good question, Doc. I'm not sure exactly what the NCAA rules say about how you should go about it, but each school is supposed to have a process for making sure the athletes know what would get them in hot water. And the schools have a vested interest in it too, to make sure they don't get put on probation. Because you know what happens then?" Miles paused for an answer, received a knowing smile and they spoke simultaneously.

"They lose money."

Miles added that he was a student representative on a student-faculty committee that provided part of the education to the students about NCAA rules.

"You're an impressive guy, Miles. I don't really think you, me, or anybody else is going to have a perfect bracket, but you have a future somewhere in all of this. Maybe you'll be NCAA president someday, if they have that kind of thing, or commissioner, whatever it's called."

Miles announced he could stay for just a few minutes more so they quickly finalized the class project strategy. First, the larger group would divide into four small groups, each filling out a bracket. Selection would be based strictly on statistics and probability, using records and measurable performance of the teams, taken from a spreadsheet that Miles had prepared. Each of the groups could add their own variables. Miles took responsibility for distributing the overall plan and explaining it to the other students. Second, Miles would take one of the brackets and use his intuition to pick at least four upsets in the first round, based on things he had heard on TV or from other people. Finally, Cusac would take Miles's bracket and fill out another one with alternative selections based on his own understanding and interpretation of variables and probability theory.

Only Cusac would submit his bracket to the actual contest, leaving the students out of it to avoid even the appearance of anything improper. The outcomes of the various brackets would ultimately be compared for educational purposes as the tournament progressed.

As they were leaving their breakfast meeting to go to the class, Cusac added as an afterthought, "I noticed that Roma had a pretty good shiner, his left eye had a nasty bruise. I guess those guys really go at it in practice, huh?"

Miles replied, "Something like that."

Cusac noted the fact that Miles had used that same phrase before when talking about Roma, and this time it seemed a little ominous, like there was something hidden behind a dark curtain.

LEARNING ABOUT LEGACY

Although they had intended their meeting on Wednesday morning to be brief, Miles and Cusac spent a full two hours in the Snack Shop. Their discussions began about Miles leading the class in making their bracket choices, but covered far more.

"I got to tell you, Doc," Miles began, "you're the teacher here, and you're the mathematician, but I still don't see how this is going to lead to a way to predict the outcomes of all these games. I just see so much, what, random things happen in these games to think predicting all of them is possible?"

Cusac smiled as he spoke, "Well, Miles, we have two possibilities. One is that you don't understand the power of statistical measurement—and just how completely and totally brilliant a mind I truly have—or the other possibility: that I don't really care if this works to predict the outcome of basketball games as long as I teach you just a little about mathematical concepts. In scientific research, far more theories are tossed out as worthless as opposed to ones that work out. But the process of study is valid just the same."

Miles smiled back. "So, I guess I'll have to wait to see if you come up with a perfect bracket to find out which of those two things is true. But tell me, are you creating a formula yourself?"

"Let's review and just leave it this way. We have the students ending up with four brackets, one from each group. I'll leave it to you to divide them into the groups. Then you will fill out your bracket using your intuition. All of these have to be finished and on my desk tomorrow before the games start. And be assured that I will submit my own bracket to the contest. I checked out the deadline, and I'll have it in. I'll probably do it in the wee hours of tonight and early tomorrow morning. Which I assume is when you and the rest of the class will be getting your brackets together too." Cusac took Miles's nodding head and two thumbs up as acknowledgment that they were on the same page.

Their hours together that Wednesday morning also allowed time for Miles to give Cusac some relevant history about Gardner-Webb basketball. Miles suggested Cusac needed this history to truly engage with the students for the class project.

"See, Doc, I grew up just a mile or so from campus and went to all the home games as far back as I can remember. So, I know the Bulldogs' basketball history."

Cusac smiled silently, appreciating that useful information was about to unfold, but also immediately aware that Miles was telling the story of his love for the team.

"So, with all the history here, and there's more than a little good stuff, the biggest story was in '07 when we beat Kentucky. I mean, sure, the Bulldogs have some impressive wins at other times, but Kentucky? I mean, Kentucky is a dynasty."

Miles paused to gauge Cusac's understanding and interest. Cusac nodded with enthusiasm, so Miles continued. "Maybe you know Dick Vitale, he's a famous sports announcer, and he always made fun of bigger teams for scheduling 'cupcake' opponents. Well, we were definitely Kentucky's cupcake that year, even though Kentucky was in a rebuilding year, only ranked number twenty in the polls."

Cusac started to ask a question but held off when Miles held up his hand to keep the floor. "So, here's how it played out. Gardner-Webb's coach, Rick Scruggs, was watching game films of Kentucky from earlier in the season. He noticed that Kentucky's opponents were timid, holding back. So, he told the Bulldogs to be aggressive and set the pace, the tempo for the game. And right out of the gate we jumped ahead, fourteen to zip."

"Zip means zero, I suppose," Cusac said with a chuckle.

"You bet, and for the first half it stayed the same, and of course at half time the announcers were pretty sure Kentucky would get it together, but no, this guy named Grayson Flittner, a guy who didn't even have a scholarship when he first came to Gardner-Webb, he just went berserk, hittin' shots from all over the court, fallin' down and ending up with maybe thirty points. He was unconscious. We won by double digits."

By the time Miles was finishing up his story, both men were bouncing up and down in their seats. When Cusac was sure the story was over, he said, "You're a great storyteller, Miles. I think I'm starting to see the story angle about why this all gets so crazy, this tournament. Got any more stories?"

"Oh yeah, let me tell you one of my favorites. Actually, it's my grandfather's favorite. The day that Artis Gilmore came to visit the campus back in the sixties. Grandpa was some kind of student assistant manager for several of the sports teams in those days.

"Artis Gilmore?" asked Cusac.

"Uh-huh, I guess I shouldn't have expected you to know that, either. Just the most famous player ever at Gardner-Webb. In the NBA Hall of Fame. Still has NBA rebounding records after all those years. But anyway, Gardner-Webb started as a junior-college—it wasn't a four-year school 'till 1971. My granddad was here before and after the change, and he was here the day in 1967 that Artis arrived for a recruiting trip to the campus."

"So, this legendary player was being recruited by Gardner-Webb. Why not the bigger schools?"

"I'm not sure I have the whole story. I'm just telling the story that my grandfather told me from his days, but the way I understand it, Artis was from a small town in Alabama, maybe Florida. But he got overlooked. What my grandfather said is that Artis had about thirty students in his high school class. They had like seven players on the basketball team."

"So, how did Gardner-Webb find him?"

"Again, part of the story I don't quite know, but Gardner-Webb did have this one supporter with money, a man named DeHart—owned a trucking company or something like that. So, Mr. DeHart, he drove down to where Artis lived. Drove his big Lincoln Continental and brought Artis up to a Gardner-Webb home game. And here's where the story gets good."

Cusac shifted to the edge of his seat. "So . . . "

"Doc, you got to stop interrupting me now. Just listen. I'm telling my grandfather's favorite story about Gardner-Webb basketball. He must have told me this story a hundred times."

Cusac held his questions and Miles continued, "So, here's the scene. Gardner-Webb had built a new student center that year, and on the front steps of the new center, half the student body was waiting there for the big limo with the next Lew Alcindor to arrive. I know you don't know who Lew Alcindor was either, but stay with me here. Well, the limo pulled up, the back door opened, and Artis stuck his long legs out of the car and stood up . . . and up . . . and up. The crowd gasped. This guy was seven feet and two inches tall."

Miles paused for dramatic effect, and Cusac pressed his index finger across his pursed lips, keeping them tightly closed but nodded to ask for more of the story. Miles happily obliged. "But here's the thing. According to Grandpa, Artis was flat terrified. Grandpa figured that the people on the steps were the biggest crowd of people Artis had ever seen in his whole life. Especially that many white people. And he was dressed in old, dirty corduroy pants that rode halfway up his calf, and he had on an old blue velour pullover sweater with one of the armpits torn out. And here's the other thing. A little later that day, Mr. DeHart took Artis to Hickory and when they came back, he had on some better clothes. Not saying anybody did anything wrong. Just sayin'."

"Wow, that's a story worth remembering. But was Artis Gardner-Webb's first black player? I have heard a little about when Duke was an all-white team," said Cusac.

"Actually, no, that's another part of the story, I guess. My grandfather used to talk about that too. They had this really fine point guard. I don't remember names, but I think he was from up north—first black player, not many in the league at that time, but a few. And you just made me remember another story. See, the black kid was not the captain of the team. The captain was a skinny white kid who was pretty much a nerd, or whatever they called the brainy guys back then, but he could really shoot. So, the story my grandfather told about him was that after Artis saw the game that night, Artis asked the skinny white kid if he thought that he could make the Gardner-Webb team. You get it? Future NBA hall of famer asking this skinny nerd if he thought he could make it at Gardner-Webb?"

"So, what did the, uh, skinny white kid tell Artis?"

Miles paused with a little smile on his lips, delaying the punch line for just a moment, then said, "So, skinny white kid tells the player who would be Gardner-Webb's best player ever—hall of fame NBA—he tells him, 'yeah, if you work really hard, you got a real shot at it.'"

Cusac and Miles laughed hard and long about the advice given to Artis. Cusac pointed to the clock on the wall. "Time to go. Time to teach you guys some math."

When Cusac arrived in the classroom, he found all his students there early, except for Simon and Roma, who had already left for the Midwest Regional where they would meet Kentucky in their first game just a few minutes after noon on Friday. Miles had run ahead of Cusac and stood at the front of the class dividing his fellow students into four groups for the purpose of creating the separate brackets. He asked them to choose a leader to present a sample of their "formulas" for characterizing a team's strengths or weaknesses, and passed out his hand-written guide about creating a final structure to make the final choices of winners of each game.

Cusac felt a surge of pride that students seemed to be fully engaged in the class project, especially given the apathetic attitudes he remembered from just days ago when he first met the class. He silently congratulated himself for following his instinct to wear his best suit for this class and look a bit less "rumpled." He positioned himself beside Miles, waited for his student to complete his organizing task, then thanked him with an overly dramatic bow.

With only a brief pause, he jumped into full teacher mode. "The word is 'equation'. Who here can define that for me?"

Rebecca, sitting in the front row with no cell phone from which to read her reply, virtually barked back the answer. "An equation is a statement, usually expressed in symbols, that the values of two mathematical expressions are equal to each other."

"I see someone has done her homework," Cusac replied, his voice carrying both praise and yet a bit of a sense of challenge. "Would you now like to tell me that you have created the kind of formula that we discussed in our last class and that you have determined how to express this as an equation?"

Rebecca smiled back at him and opened her mouth to speak but before words came, he held up his hand, "No. I can see from your expression that indeed you have, so let's let someone else speak now. Anyone else?"

From the back of the room, a student gave a timid reply. "Well . . . I figured out what . . . I think . . . you wanted in a formula, but I don't exactly know what to do with it . . . I mean, I haven't exactly figured out the difference between a formula and an equation . . . I mean, I don't know how they fit together, actually."

"Good enough. Let's start with your formula. Please give me the factors that are available for statistical measurement that, when combined, may add up to some opportunity for predicting a successful performance of a basketball team."

"Well . . . okay . . . I took the won-loss record . . . and the point differential . . . that's what we talked about last time. Then I looked at whether a team won their conference tournament, but with that I'm having a hard time figuring what kind of number to give it. It's really a yes or no kind of factor."

Cusac turned to Rebecca. "Help your classmate out, Rebecca."

"Easy. Just decide in your mind how important you think winning the conference tournament is, and give it a number. Maybe just a one or a two. You can always adjust it later if you decide it's more or less important."

"Wow," Cusac exulted. "Rebecca, you have earned yourself a place at the head of the class. Pull your desk up here and turn it around to face the others." Rebecca hesitated, unsure if he was serious, then quickly did as she was told. She sat beaming, looking at the rest of her classmates.

"And your fourth factor?" Cusac returned his focus to the other student.

"The coach. Has the coach ever won a national championship? So . . . I had the same question there, about how to turn it into a measurable number . . . so, do I just give it a number depending on how important I think it is?"

"There's learning going on here!" Cusac announced, punching the air with his finger. "We now have four elements predictive of future success that we can measure. Won-loss record, a number that indicates the relative dominance over other teams they have played, recent success in a tournament playoff situation, and the value of proven leadership. Anyone want to quibble with those selections?"

Another student spoke up with a challenge: "I get that so far, but some things you just can't measure like that. Like if a team started out with a really great year and just faded over the course of the year, just sorta burned out, got tired, maybe. And another team that lost a lot at the first of the year but gets it together. They got the same record, but one's just playing together better at the end of the year."

"Rebecca?" Cusac prompted. "You want to handle that?"

"Sure. There's a word for that. It's called 'momentum'."

Cusac shot back, "Give me a way to measure momentum."

"Divide up the season into thirds or fourths. See the one in which they had the best won-loss and point differential. If the fourth is better than the previous ones, give them a positive number, if not, give them a minus number. Maybe give them extra points if they have a real winning streak going into the tournament."

Cusac paced, virtually strutted around the class, again praising Rebecca, then asking for more elements to measure. Some students came up with useful ideas, others offered humorous suggestions, such as whether a team's mascot is a predator, such as an alligator, as opposed to a song-bird like a cardinal. Alternatively, how about if the bird is an eagle? And, *What in the world is a Crimson Tide?*

Cusac surprised the class by endorsing or at least encouraging discussion of some of the obscure offerings. He added his own surprising measure. "So, if your team's mascot is a native American tribe, and you are playing a team that is, for instance, a wolf, how does that work?"

Miles put in, "You're kidding, aren't you?"

"Maybe I'm just trying to be funny, maybe I'm just saying there is a possibility here that has never been studied. Here's the thing: I heard on the TV last night that teams wearing red have had a statistically significant advantage over teams wearing blue. So, maybe we have some things that at first sound silly but, in reality, are important but have never been field-tested. I'm just saying, you can put anything you want in your formula and see where it gets you."

The class grew silent, but only briefly, as Cusac again took control of the discussion. "But still, with all this we've still only talked about formulas. How do we get to the equation part?"

Rebecca raised her right hand, but held her other hand over her mouth, indicating that she wanted to speak, but would not do so without permission. Cusac laughed as he replied, "Okay, Rebecca, go ahead. Unless there is someone else who wants to challenge your ascendance to assistant professor."

Rebecca took a quick glance around the room, and seeing no one eager to reply, she slowly described how to put formula together with equation. "The formula gets you half the way there. The formula grants you a numerical score that may be considered the overall value or talent of one team. But you then have to compare two teams to see which one has the better chance of coming out on top of the other."

Rebecca took a quick glance at Cusac, who was nodding slowly, then continued. "So, assign a score to each team, put each score on opposite sides of the equal sign, and whoever has the highest score is the one most likely to win."

With Rebecca's simple description of how to complete the calculations to measure each team against the opponent, the necessary work became clear. With Miles taking notes about who would populate the several work groups, the plan to apply the measurements to predictions and then make bracket selections was completed.

Miles ended with a summary. "You all know how much work we have to do. The small groups will pretty much take all afternoon to do your scores, based on what formulas you end up with. Then we'll need to meet tonight in Bost Gym. You know I have a key, yes? We'll be there late. Everybody okay with this? Seven? Seven-thirty?" Cusac was pretty sure he saw enthusiasm in the faces of his students but was surprised when they all clapped hands with thirty seconds of applause.

THE PLAN GETS
COMPLICATED

O n Wednesday morning, Sinclair stood in the doorway of the conference room, observing the various members of the Consortium work their magic. She was particularly drawn to the way Marilyn, her social media expert, led her group. She watched Marilyn move among the small working groups of two to four people, gently touching some of them on the forearm or shoulder while she pointed at the computer screens and asked questions. Each staff member seemed to welcome the interactions, the touch, and they returned smiles. The groups sometimes broke out in brief, controlled laughter. Sinclair couldn't help but marvel at the visual contrast between the very conservative looking Marilyn and the heavily tattooed Lilith, but there clearly was a comfort and warmth between them.

This is how a mother treats her children, Sinclair mused, and searched her memory for times that she received from her own mother such gentle touches and encouraging smiles. There was precious little to remember. Sinclair reflected on something a therapist had once said about her mother—actually, about both of her parents. "Everything was always about them."

Sinclair still felt pride in each of her parents' social and academic accomplishments and felt grateful that their money had sent her to the best schools, but *everything was always about them*. A sense of dread, almost panic, welled up inside. She felt overwhelmed by the project, responsible for the success of something big, and for the people in the room.

She silently questioned the wisdom of leaving a good paying job where she worked under the supervision of others who were older and more powerful than she. A single word crept into her mind: *Imposter. That's me. I'm just an imposter here.*

"Sinclair! Sinclair, can you come over here for a minute?" Marilyn's voice called Sinclair out of her reverie. "We have something here you need to look at."

They huddled around a screen showing a YouTube video. A middle-aged black man, easily the oldest of Marilyn's team, explained, "I just wanted to show you what we worked out with the guy doing the trick basketball shots. It looks pretty good."

"Isn't it a little late?" Sinclair asked.

"No, I don't think so. It's been up twenty-four hours, but it's just now gone viral. If you track the timing of entry fees coming in, you could make the argument that it accelerated entries by maybe twenty percent. But it's hard to be sure. We're still fishing for entries, and we'll get a better count when the deadline passes."

Marilyn patted the man gently on the back. "Joel, you did a great job with this." She turned to the others and added, "Joel handled the whole thing. Negotiated the contract with the guy and modified the content in just over eight hours. Let's watch."

The screen filled up with ninety seconds of unbelievable trick basketball shots, some banking off walls, others through the scaffolding of rafters, and simpler shots but with the shooter blindfolded. Crawling across the screen ran the messages calling the viewer to enter the contest: *Billion Dollar Bracket—Take the*

Shot—You Can't Win if You Don't Shoot—Dream Big—Beat the
Odds—Billion Dollar Bracket.

"And you say we paid him just five hundred dollars? I mean this is a real attention grabber, and a perfect fit for our hook."

Marilyn smiled. "Maybe you'll approve a little bonus for him when it's all over."

"That's good. That's great," said Sinclair. She reached to Joel for a traditional handshake, which he turned into a high-five and a fist bump, Sinclair's first. "What else can you show me?"

For another thirty minutes, the social media team laid out how they were using Facebook, Twitter, and other media to spread the word. Sinclair's familiarity with this world was superficial, but she felt she at least did not embarrass herself during the tour.

Most of the morning her own silenced phone had been buzzing with a number she did not recognize. She did not answer because she feared it would be someone from the media wanting to talk about the contest. But now she saw that the same number had left multiple messages. She stepped outside the room and opened up the last message.

"This is Montevista Hospital emergency room. If this is the number for Sinclair Dane, please call me immediately."

Sinclair knew it had to be about her mother. She ran to her car before she returned the call. After a long wait on hold with the emergency room, a nurse finally came on the line.

"This is Marie. Is this Sinclair Dane?"

"Yes it is. Is this about my mother, Lillian?"

"Yes. We found some papers on her and I think that's what it meant. She was brought here this morning. Can you come over as quickly as possible?"

Sinclair replied with panic in her voice, "I can. But tell me about my mother."

"We really don't like to talk on the phone about—"

"Is she dead?" Sinclair sobbed into the phone.

The nurse understood Sinclair's level of distress, and added, "No, wait. Your mother is not dead. But she's hurt. I don't know how far away you are, but don't rush. Take your time. Don't hurry, just come as soon as you can. It's about permission for surgery."

"Surgery! What kind of surgery?" she screamed into the phone.

The nurse remained calm and professional. "Please. Just come. She's going to be okay. Just come on."

Sinclair roared out of her parking place then realized she could not see through her tears. She stopped the car and pulled back to the curb. She dried her eyes and spoke out loud. "Don't rush. She's okay." She pounded her fists on the steering wheel. "This can't happen now! I've done so much for her! I've tried so hard! God damn it. God damn it. God damn it!"

Five minutes later, she pulled out of the parking lot to go to the hospital.

REBECCA

C usac settled into bed Wednesday night in his own apartment, exhausted from teaching and the stress of what he had to learn to be able to meet his responsibility for Cheeky. A family friend agreed to stay over at Donna's house so Cusac could have a night away. He had chosen a place to live within walking distance of the campus, and he now felt the first feeling of pleasure at how he had arranged his new living space. It occurred to him to have Cheeky over soon, because she would eventually be living there with him.

Before turning out the light, he read a collection of newspaper articles and a few narrative paragraphs that Miles had given to him in the Snack Shop earlier that day. Miles had described some of the material as a draft of the history of the basketball team. Taken collectively, they added information and gave recent context to the other things Miles had described about the history of Gardner-Webb basketball.

"In 2002, scandal rocked the small Christian School of about 4,000 students. The college president was found to have had a hand in altering the grade of an athlete in order to keep him eligible. As the story unfolded, strife and conflict tore the administration apart, and the customarily peaceful student body marched in the streets holding up copies of the student honor code. After an investigation, the governing body of intercollegiate sports, the National Collegiate Athletic Association, made the decision to place the basketball team on probation for five years."

Cusac found the information from Miles interesting, but with work to do to finish his bracket, he scanned or skipped most of the material. One section did catch his eye, mostly because it was about Simon.

"This year's team struggled at the first of the season, unable to carve out the appropriate role for the player who was so clearly the dominant athlete on the team. The other four starters were seniors and, although capable athletes, none anticipated a future in professional basketball. Their collective resentment for the young superstar affected the team's play until, led by Roma Hill, a late-night, players-only team meeting took place, excluding Simon Bradley. For over an hour, they argued and soul-searched, coming to the logical conclusion that if they wanted to win basketball games, they needed to get over their own egos and "release the beast" known as Simon Bradley. It worked. They had lost the first eight conference games, sometimes by just a few points, but after that meeting, they won the last ten and made it into the national tournament by winning their conference tournament. The lesser talented players of the team, collectively and individually, found a way to make peace with being the supporting cast to the future millionaire in their midst.

When national media finally discovered Simon Bradley, the inevitable question always came: Why Gardner-Webb? This talented athlete was not really an unknown quantity; he had offers from all the big-name schools, including all of the NCAA tournament winners of the last ten years. The accepted story is that it was a family issue. The small-town life and the Christian values of Gardner-Webb replicated his growing up years in Australia. Gardner-Webb would be just the right place for him to spend one year playing college basketball and then sign the professional basketball contract that would ultimately make him a very rich man.

Despite the talent of Simon Bradley and the supporting play of Roma Hill at point guard, the NCAA tournament selection committee still found Gardner-Webb worthy of only a number sixteen seeding in the brackets. Furthermore, the committee could not resist the temptation to match Gardner-Webb with the number one seed in the tournament: Kentucky."

As Cusac finished his reading, he dozed off in the lighted bedroom. Miles's papers still lay scattered on the bed beside him. He awoke startled by a loud knock on the door. For a moment he felt disoriented and spilled the papers off the bed onto the floor. It took him a moment to remember why the room was lit and what he had been doing before falling asleep. He quickly dressed and staggered to answer the door. His mind raced with fears about some catastrophe with Cheeky's mother.

Opening the door, he found Rebecca clutching an armful of notebooks and various papers, a writing pen in her mouth. Her hair was tangled and she wore mismatched gym clothes.

She rushed past him into the room before he could speak.

"I need your help," she blurted out breathlessly and began to spread out several groupings of papers on the floor of the living room. "I just came from the meeting, and—and those people are going nowhere. They don't get it! I've tried to be patient with them but—but here's what I've got. I've got a formula here with sixty-one variables—and I think it's almost done—but I do need your help. Is this enough? Will it fly?" She frantically shuffled papers one pile to another while speaking, more to herself than to Cusac.

Overwhelmed by Rebecca's dramatic entry and obviously frantic state of mind, Cusac struggled to know how to answer. He responded to the one factual statement she made. "You have a formula with sixty-one elements . . . uh . . . variables?"

"Sixty-one. I think it's enough, although I ruled out a dozen more because they're so complicated, and I just don't have any confidence in how to make the calculations, but I think it's enough without them. I can let you see them if you want. But I think it's enough, sixty-one. I mean, everyone else was just picking six or seven—maybe a few had ten—and that's nowhere near enough to really match teams up. And everyone was stuck, just stuck on this thing they were calling strength of schedule. Sure, I get it, some teams don't play the best other teams and some do, but I figure it's not about—or I should say it's such a small part of what a team can do when they do play the better teams—"

"Rebecca, how did you know where I live?"

Rebecca seemed shocked to be interrupted with a change of topic and paused just a moment before answering. "So, I went over to where your—what—niece and that little girl lives, the one you told us about, and like, there was this other woman there and, sure, she told me I should not come here in the middle of the night, but I wouldn't leave until she told me where you were and, sure, I promised her I wouldn't come, at least until morning. She said she was going to call you, but I guess it's so late she didn't. But that's not the point. This stuff has to be on your desk in a few hours, and so what was I supposed to do?"

Just then came another knock on the door. Cusac returned to the door and allowed Miles and another female classmate into the room. "Hi Rebecca. Can we talk?" asked Miles as he slowly crossed the room, hands in pockets, speaking softly.

By this time, Cusac had figured out what had happened. While he had no personal experience with students with emotional breakdowns, he was aware of a number of such situations with students at Duke. Rebecca became silent and looked at each of the others in turn and eventually asked simply, "Am I in trouble?"

Miles motioned for Cusac to follow him into an adjoining room, leaving the two women students alone in conversation. Miles explained, "Rebecca's parents are on the way here. They are driving over from Charlotte. It's less than an hour. Rebecca has done this a couple of times, and we have a plan for her. Her parents will take her to a hospital, and she'll get straightened out in a week or so. The plan worked fine the last time we had to do it. Not so much the first time. But we saw it coming by the end of class today. Actually, I wondered about it after the first class, the one on Monday."

"Did I do something . . . wrong, to cause this?" Cusac asked timidly.

"No, not really, but Rebecca is impressed with status and power. The way you ran the class seemed to strike her as you being something really different and special. Which I guess you are, but whatever. I think it was your confidence and the Duke thing. I mean, we have great teachers here . . . but you see what I mean? Anyway, as best we can put it all together, Rebecca hasn't slept since that first class. Up two nights straight just obsessing over formulas and the bracket thing. She walked into the meeting tonight with the most garbled gobbledygook you've ever heard, and we had work to do and . . . so . . . she didn't take it well when somebody suggested she was going off the rails a bit. Maybe we weren't very tactful. Not everybody is patient with her when she gets like this. So, we guessed right about where she would go and we followed her over here. I'm sorry it got to this point and that she woke you up."

An hour-plus later, after rounds of ice water and lemonade for all, Rebecca accepted the advice and guidance of her parents who, along with the female classmate, left for a planned admission to a psychiatric hospital. Miles and Cusac looked briefly through the papers Rebecca had assembled. An incomprehensible array of Greek and Latin letters, Egyptian hieroglyphics and other unidentifiable artistic constructions dominated the writing, punctuated with stars and exclamation points. She had written the word "Eureka" in bold red letters, all caps, multiple times.

After Miles left, Cusac found himself wide awake after midnight but at the same time exhausted. What he needed to do for the bracket alternated with waves of guilt and fear that he might be held responsible for Rebecca's crisis. For now, she was in the custody of her parents and headed to a hospital, but he felt he needed to do more to help her, but what?

A profound sense of doubt invaded his thoughts that he would be able to manage the far more complex duty of caring for Cheeky for the rest of her life. Or his.

THE REMATCH

Despite Rebecca's troubles, the other students completed their work, creating four separate bracket choices, and placed them on Cusac's desk Thursday morning. Miles added his alternative entry, using his intuition beyond variables, formulas, and equations. Cusac had worked the rest of the night, barely sleeping two hours, before submitting the lone actual entry into the contest an hour before the deadline that same morning. He paid the $2 entry fee using an app called *Ring-It* that Miles had helped him download to his smartphone. Borderline exhausted from the events with Rebecca and with Cheeky, he felt little excitement or anticipation about either the contest or the class activities.

The first-round game between the Gardner-Webb Running Bulldogs and the Kentucky Wildcats took place early Friday afternoon. Despite the traditional neutral court scheduling for the tournament, a complicated set of scheduling circumstances put the game in Rupp Arena, the site of the 2007 upset of Kentucky by Gardner-Webb.

Kentucky blue filled 95 percent of the seats in the arena. Gardner-Webb's red and black clustered mainly around their bench. Deafening pregame noise from fans, bands, and homemade devices drowned out the sports announcers' customary court level interviews. One commentator gave up and mouthed to the camera that she would try her interview again at half-time. "Wildcat Nation" thus assembled for the empire to strike back.

Simon Bradley took his place at center-court for the opening tip against his virtual double, in performance statistics and in many other physical characteristics. The Kentucky center also stood tall as one of the remarkably talented freshmen expected to jump to professional basketball after one year in college. His scoring average of 14 points per game did not match Simon Bradley's only because Kentucky fielded three other equally talented Wildcat teammates who shared the Wildcats' offensive production. Gardner-Webb faced an opponent with at least four, if not five, professional basketball superstars and future millionaires. Some would someday have athletic shoes named for them.

Simon out-jumped his rival for the opening tip-off and guided it to Roma Hill, who sprinted with the ball to the far-left corner of the court. Simon wheeled and raced to the basket. Roma sent a high-arching pass in the direction of the rim. Simon leapt high in the air, caught it cleanly and dunked it softly, showing restraint of emotion, exhibiting grace rather than power. The Kentucky center reacted quickly but trailed Simon by a full step. In a hurry to defend the basket, he slammed into Simon while he was still in the air, cutting his legs out from under him and spinning Simon into a full 360-degree backflip. Simon landed on two feet and two hands, catlike and unharmed, looking directly into the face of the player who had upended him. With surprise, anger, and confusion showing on his face, the Kentucky center added to the harm by impulsively head-butting Simon in front of millions of television viewers.

The referees' whistles blew the crowd silent. A quick conference of all officials at the scorer's table determined that two flagrant fouls would be assessed on the Kentucky center, one for undercutting Simon, the other for the head butt. Kentucky's best player was ejected from the game. The game clock had ticked off only five seconds.

In an arena as silent as an abandoned cathedral, Simon Bradley sank the four free throws to which he was entitled, two for each of the fouls. Gardner-Webb then took the ball out of bounds. Roma Hill quickly swished a three-point shot from the top of the key, and the score was nine to zero, eleven seconds into the game. After several trips up and down the court with no one scoring, it also became clear that Kentucky was trying to hide the fact that their own point guard had been injured the day before in practice. He was bravely trying to play with a heavily taped ankle sprain, and he was in obvious pain. Kentucky called time out, and their second-best player was taken to the locker room. The game was now two minutes old.

Kentucky did not quit. Their considerable talent in the other starters and from the bench made the game competitive. But Gardner-Webb had Simon Bradley. He scored from every spot on the court. On defense he blocked one shot after another, usually keeping the ball in play for a fast break for Gardner-Webb, rather than swatting it into the stands. Simon fielded passes from Roma and slammed them to the bottom of the basket. He set up in the corner for three-point scores, and he ran the court on fast breaks that ended in easy layups for him or his teammates. The tall, talented teenager from Australia broke the hearts of Kentucky fans.

Early in the second half of the game, Kentucky gave up trying to guard Simon one-to-one and had two players shadowing him constantly, at every opportunity trying to jump in front of him and foul him out with charging infractions. At each attempt, Simon avoided the direct contact just enough for the fouls to go against Kentucky. Less than eight minutes into the second half, four of the Wildcats had fouled out trying to guard him.

By the end of the game, Simon Bradley had scored 68 points

in a 106–91 win over the undefeated and top-ranked Kentucky Wildcats. Roma Hill delivered 22 assists. The Gardner-Webb coach, struggling for words to describe what his team had just accomplished, stated flatly in the after-game press conference, "I've coached him for a year, and I had no idea Simon was that good."

Back in Boiling Springs, North Carolina, the Gardner-Webb campus exploded with joy. A big screen television had been set up in the old intramural Bost Gymnasium for students to gather and participate in what most thought would be a short ride in the tournament. Even so, most classes that day had continued uninterrupted. Barely one hundred students milled around in Bost Gym at the start of the game. By the end of the game, the story had spread and students were streaming out of dorms and classrooms headed to Paul Porter Arena, the larger venue, for a full-tilt pep rally celebration. Some pumped their fists in celebration, some seemed to want to touch anyone they could reach, slapping each others' hands and giving hugs to anyone who would slow down enough to allow it. Many looked shocked, not really ready to believe what just happened.

Neither ESPN nor any local station had thought to assign a reporter or camera to the Gardner-Webb campus for the human-interest stories that sometimes accompany the games' broadcast. By the time the incomprehensible upset was completed, TV-crew trucks raced toward Boiling Springs from Charlotte's two main broadcast stations.

Cusac, still exhausted from his duties with Cheeky and the incident with Rebecca, had lost track of time and essentially forgot when the game had been scheduled, or rather never bothered to find out when it would be played. Throughout the morning, he spent several hours alone, trying to anticipate what he should do next. He returned to an old habit, making lists, and tried to structure his thoughts that way. Nothing made it on to the page. Still worried about what might happen with Rebecca, and even more anxious about his future with Cheeky, he wished he could cry, then scolded himself for the thought.

At the time of the game, he sat with Cheeky and Davita Thompson at her school, playing rhyming games. Before and after her lesson, he tried to open a conversation with Cheeky about her mother's deteriorating health. He found her unwilling or unable to talk about it. Davita Thompson told him she would try to help next time, and they scheduled another tutoring session that would be focused on helping Cheeky express herself about her mother. Cheeky and Cusac returned home to a house filled with gloom and silence.

The following morning during breakfast, Cusac turned on the television and learned the outcome of the game. He smiled and said softly to himself, "Well, how about that." He wondered how many of the games he predicted wrongly but had no time to check. It was time to take Cheeky's mother to a Saturday morning doctor's appointment.

Sinclair Dane also missed all the basketball games that afternoon. She stayed at the hospital where her mother had been taken after she was found on the street, beaten and bloody. She sat across the room and cried as she watched her mother sleep, after the surgeons had finished setting several broken bones and addressing other injuries. One of the older woman's eyes was bandaged shut. A patch of hair was missing from the left side of her head. A television set hung on the wall in the hospital room. It never occurred to Sinclair to turn it on.

As Sinclair sat beside the bed and noted the skin wrinkle lines, whitening hair and other features of aging in her mother, her own obsessive fear struck her mind and heart. She looked at the woman in the bed and saw her future self. Despite reassurances from her own psychotherapist and several doctors that this was almost certainly not to be her fate, she believed this would be how her life would end. Psychotic. Alone. Like so many of the women in her family.

The members of The Consortium who had remained at the war room—those who were not sleeping off forty-eight hours of dedication to their respective tasks—puzzled over whether or not Gardner-Webb's upset over Kentucky was good news or bad for the Billion Dollar Bracket Contest. The past two days had been a frenzy of receiving contest entries, selling contracts for advertising on their web site, and placing their own posts on social media.

Kentucky's defeat surely meant there would be no perfect bracket, but presuming that all brackets were busted and no one still perfect so early, that probably meant the plans for advertising revenue were dead. Alinsky sat alone in a corner furiously punching numbers into a laptop. He wore a serious, angry look on his face. No one dared interrupt him.

TWO PERFECT BRACKETS

Cusac and Cheeky spent most of Saturday together. In the morning, they worked on some of Cheeky's homework assignments. Cusac found their interactions more comfortable and rewarding than he anticipated, even though he had never worked with a student this young or one with her limitations. Feeling frustrated at times when she didn't quickly grasp tasks that seemed very obvious, he promised himself he would learn more about children with special learning needs.

After the schoolwork, they walked around outside on a surprisingly warm March day. Finding some early blooms on some of the plants in the backyard, Cusac wished he knew more about flowers to teach her about that.

Cheeky's mother slept peacefully in her bedroom. Cheeky knew Davita Thompson would be coming by after lunch for a special visit. But when she arrived at the door, Cheeky ran crying to her room.

"What was she told about why I was coming?" Ms. Thompson asked.

"I just said you were coming to talk about the nurse who was going to be helping Donna," Cusac replied defensively, with both fatigue and frustration showing in his voice.

"The hospice nurse. Yes. We did say we would talk to her about that. What does Cheeky know about her?"

Cusac walked back into the living room, sat down hard in a chair and covered his face with his hands. He sighed deeply. "Nothing. I told her almost nothing. She didn't want to hear anything. But I think she heard me on the phone. She won't talk and doesn't ask about any of this."

Ms. Thompson smiled. "Little girl's got big ears. Probably trying to put together bits and pieces she's heard and resisting it too. Probably seems mysterious to her. Maybe it's time to be really direct."

Ms. Thompson walked to Cheeky's door, which she had not closed, and asked if she could come in. Cusac checked his phone and shuffled some work papers but found he had trouble focusing on anything. Ten minutes later, they joined Cusac at the dining room table.

Ms. Thompson surprised Cusac with the directness of her question. "Cheeky, what do you know about dying?"

Cheeky surprised Cusac with the directness of her answer. "Plants die. Cats die. Trees die, and people come and cut them down and you never see them again."

"Wow, you know a lot, girl," Ms. Thompson came back. And waited.

Cheeky sat still and relaxed, but a reddening face and tearful eyes betrayed her emotion. "And I know that people die."

"And you know that your mommy is going to die?"

Cheeky nodded and the tears came, but she stayed calm and started another question. "When will she . . . just . . . " She could not finish.

"I think you will have a lot of questions, Cheeky, but I want you to know a few things. We have this really nice lady who is a nurse who will come in and help us all."

Cusac finally spoke. "And I hear that she is really good about answering questions. Everybody always has a lot of questions when people die, and I bet you have a lot of them."

"I want to know when Mommy can talk to me."

"Hey. I think that's a good idea. She will probably sleep a little more today, then we'll see if she will get up and eat with us."

Ms. Thompson added, "And maybe that's enough questions for today. Want to go with me to the store? I have to buy some stuff. I could use the help."

Cusac watched them leave, relieved that there was someone who knew how to do this and was willing to help. The basketball tournament and the students were always in the back of his mind but a distant second to Cheeky's needs. He went to check on Donna, who was still sleeping soundly. He stretched out on the couch and caught up on his own sleep deficit. Sunday brought more of the same, with the Hospice nurse taking over Donna's care and quiet, peaceful moments with Cheeky.

On Monday morning after Cheeky had left for school, and with the hospice nurse performing her duties with her patient, Cusac turned his attention back to basketball and the math class he would be conducting later that morning. He clicked on the television to hear the ESPN announcers say that order had been restored to the world of collegiate basketball, with Gardner-Webb losing to Dayton in the second round of games on Sunday. Colorful metaphors flowed, primarily the obvious one that "Cinderella's dance was a short one." One commentator added that Simon Bradley's forty-six points in the second game added up to an all-time scoring record for the first two games of the tournament and that, despite the loss, he probably played himself into being a first-round pick in the NBA draft.

Cusac picked up the morning copy of *The Charlotte Observer* and opened the sports section to review how many of the games he had correctly predicted. Comparing the scores to his own bracket, he one by one checked off game after game as correct. When he finished, and when he had rechecked the information twice, he leaned back in his chair and said softly to himself, "Wow. Who would have thought? Class will certainly be interesting. I need to get going."

He rushed to finish dressing and left for his class, turning off the television before he heard the ESPN announcers say, "And on a sidenote, despite the loss by Kentucky, the Billion Dollar Bracket Contest is still alive with two perfect brackets. We're trying to get in touch with the holders of the brackets, and we'll keep you up to date on this part of the story."

Back at the Consortium war room Monday morning, bedlam had returned. Sinclair Dane was in the middle of an emotional meltdown, screaming into the phone: "I don't care when your fuckin' plane leaves or where it's going. Get your ass back here, now! We have two perfect brackets, and we need you! Right now!" She turned to those still in the room with her and blurted out a series of marginally understandable orders to those involved in the advertising part of their strategy.

"Don't we need to know who these people are? The ones with the perfect scores?" someone asked.

"Of course we know who they are. Do you think I'm stupid? That I haven't looked at our database? One of them is someone with a history. Joel, have you found out any more about her?"

"Oh, yeah. She's got her own Wiki page, and you're not gonna believe why. She's one of that small group of remarkable people who has won big gambling jackpots—not once, but twice."

Rod Browning and Marilyn spoke simultaneously, "That doesn't sound good."

Sinclair answered calmly, a marked contrast to her demeanor just a few minutes earlier, "Maybe. Maybe not. She's still not home free, and we might be able to market her fame into more advertising for us. What else does the Wiki page say?"

Joel picked up the narrative. "Okay, I'm reading here. Hazel Grithens grew up as the only daughter of a rural African American Christian evangelist. She spent her childhood years washing the feet of supplicant sinners at her father's lucrative tent revivals. First attending public school in her teen years, she was discovered to have an IQ in excess of 200. She graduated from law school at age twenty-two."

"Oh, hell," spoke one of Marilyn's team, "we got ourselves a flippin' genius with a track record of winning $1M jackpots, and now she's goin' for the $1B."

Sinclair again cautioned the others, "Keep in mind that prediction is most difficult after the first rounds. More evenly matched teams. No easy picks. Joel, is there information on the contests she won?"

"Lots. I'll paraphrase it. First win in Vegas, accused of cheating, charges dropped, walked away with $2M and a ton of notoriety. Never practiced law, gave away all her winnings and disappeared from public view for twelve years. Spent that time cleaning houses for rich people in Durham, and then re-emerged in 2003 when she won the NC Education Lottery, $8M. Gave away most of it and that's where the page ends. Looks like she disappeared again after winning the lottery."

The entire group sat in silence. Even Sinclair needed a moment to take in the information about this unusual turn of events and the unusual person that was Hazel Grithens. The clickety-click of Joel's keyboard broke the silence.

Rod spoke first. "Hey, I could be wrong here, but I've got a feeling that we're going to hear more from Hazel Grithens."

Joel replied, as he continued to work his keyboard, "Got that right. Monday morning is not over yet, and she's already on television giving interviews."

"Is she on ESPN?" asked Rod.

"No. She's on Bloomberg Television," Joel replied with a chuckle.

"Bloomberg what? What?" asked several puzzled staff members.

Rod picked up the conversation. "I hope everybody here can see what's getting ready to happen here. Bloomberg makes perfect sense. It's about money. This woman's not done."

"But why Bloomberg? It's pretty much straight news, not a lot of glitz," Sinclair said.

"Who knows?" Rod came back. "She's a puzzle. Maybe she's got connections in the money world. Maybe she didn't give away all that money after all. But I'm guessing we're going to get another chapter in this woman's remarkable life. She's not done. And I can't wait to see what she comes up with."

"The real point is what can *we* come up with," Sinclair added. "If this becomes a story, then it's more eyes on our website, more eyes on all those banner ads, and more money for us. Do we know what she's saying on the Bloomberg interview?"

Only fifteen minutes passed before the Hazel Grithens interview rotated through the morning newsfeed on Bloomberg Television. Sinclair's group watched in silence as the interviewer welcomed a small, thin, conservatively dressed, and groomed middle-aged black woman to the set. But when Hazel spoke, the room sparkled. Her total-face smile, her glistening white teeth, and her enthusiasm, took over the moment.

"Yes, I am back. I am back to give away another fortune. And I am going to win $1B and give it all away. And I'm going to give a lot of it away before I win it." Her words betrayed little emotion beyond a cheerful and positive attitude. Her smile seemed to grow larger with each moment that passed.

The sharp-dressed Bloomberg staff reporter spoke with a decidedly British accent as he structured the piece. "Now, our viewers may need a little background here. You have won and given away prize money earnings before?"

"Yes, but I don't want to talk about what I have done in the past. I want to talk about the future. If you want to know more about my past, then go to my website. I think you have that scrolling across the screen right now."

"What does the future hold, Ms. Grithens?"

"Well, let me just add that some people in your world, your world of finance, sir, know me and know that I have a modest little investment account. It's time to give it all away and roll into it the $1B that I will soon win. I'm going to invest what I have now in a telethon to raise money for college scholarships."

At that point in the interview, Hazel stood up, stretched out her arms, lifted her face to the heavens, and virtually sang her next words. "I am going to raise money for the poor kids who can't afford college! North Carolina has all these wonderful colleges that used to be schools for blacks, what you call the historically black schools. They need money!"

The interviewer looked momentarily speechless, but quickly recovered. "And how will we learn about your plan for the telethon, Ms. Grithens?"

"Go to the website! It's on the screen!" Hazel rocked in rhythm to music that only she could hear, and beamed out her smile to the camera that moved in for a close-up. She added, "Keep your eyes open for opportunity to give to poor college kids, yellow and brown, black and white. All are precious in His sight. Thank you, Lord-of-us-all. Bless our work for poor kids."

After a few seconds, the camera switched back to the interviewer.

"That's all of that for now. When we come back, an update on today's market. This is Bloomberg Television."

A truly stunned and silent Consortium war room slowly found a way back to work on the ads that would now flow, thanks to the momentum that perfect brackets would now provide. With his back to the others in the room, Alinsky stared into his smartphone and smiled.

THE BIG REVEAL

C usac's Monday morning math class was ten minutes along by the time ESPN and other outlets reported the full story of the two perfect bracket entries. He had been successful in requiring all electronic devices to be turned off, so no one knew that he had a perfect bracket. He hid his own excitement from the unsuspecting students, downplaying this in anticipation of enjoying a dramatic moment of revelation.

A third of the class was absent, including Roma Hill and Simon Bradley. Those who were there seemed depressed or simply exhausted after the roller coaster of the win over Kentucky and the loss to Dayton.

"Okay, I know all of you must be worn out with the Gardner-Webb part of the tournament, but we're back in learning mode now, and we have some interesting things to discuss—about math! Remember? This is not really about basketball. It's about what you can learn about mathematics through basketball."

A sleepy and silent group of students looked blankly at Cusac. There was no Rebecca to pick up the conversation. She remained hospitalized. The students who knew her best felt an enduring sadness about her troubles, adding to the gloom.

"As you all know, we have four primary brackets to review," Cusac began. He turned away and taped summaries of the brackets from the groups to the board at the front of the class. "The final score for each bracket is written at the top in red. I think it's big enough for you to see. Feel free to come up closer if you want the details." He paused while the students examined the results.

"So, it's a tie," one student spoke. "Every bracket had ten or eleven wrong, except the one that missed thirteen. That's terrible." The class collectively laughed at their failure to predict at a higher level.

"Is it? Is it bad? What if you compare it to a coin flip? Which would probably get half or so wrong. Looks to me like considering variables in a thoughtful way did pretty well."

Cusac took the next half hour to point out examples of where formulas they had developed did not work, and a few places where they did. There were eight games that were considered upsets based on their seeding, including the Gardner-Webb upset. All four brackets had picked at least one of the upsets.

"That's beautiful!" Cusac erupted with more emotion than the students had seen in him before. "You took data and put it into a formula and predicted upsets. You did better than the Las Vegas oddsmakers! Do you get it? Am I making sense? Data. Information. Formulas!"

Several students laughed at the sight of Cusac standing in front of the room, his arms stretched out and knees bent like he was in a basketball defensive stance. Gradually, it seemed to sink in to the students that there was something to learn in the numbers.

"Now we will have Miles give his picks, and I think you will remember he was to go with his gut and pick some upsets based not on formulas but his overall understanding of the game." The class again chuckled softly as they saw that Miles's bracket had twelve errors, with only one of the "intuitive" upsets he predicted coming through.

Miles defended himself. "The twelve seeds didn't give me any wins over the fives. And no one that was seeded a ten or a nine beat anyone. That's ridiculous! Not supposed to happen!"

Cusac turned to Miles with a smirk and said, "Breathe in, breathe out, Miles. It's gonna be okay."

Finally, Cusac handed out copies of his bracket and asked the students to compare them to the actual winners; he calmly waited for the results to sink in. Up to that point, Cusac had sensed that the energy from the class was starting to wane, with all the negative results and the discussions focused on math concepts.

At first the class grew more silent, until Miles spoke. "Uh . . . uh . . . is this your real bracket? I, uh, is this the bracket you actually sent in?"

"Yes," Cusac deadpanned, then allowed a smile.

Several screamed out loud. Some rushed the front of the room for high fives and pats on the back. Others applauded. "Way to go, Doc!"

Cusac, overwhelmed, tried to first thank them then scold them back to their seats, asking a generally stated question. He tried without success to direct them back to a discussion about what one could learn from a comparison of the brackets. But the students were not going along with this, and those who had cell phones and laptops brought them online to spread the news. Any semblance of a class in session vanished.

As the students milled around the room, several saw through the classroom window that a large number of people were gathering outside the building. Someone pointed out that the crowd included what looked like TV cameras. Cusac ultimately gave up on holding the class, quickly packed his briefcase, and tried unsuccessfully to exit the building. A mass of students and media trapped Cusac against a side door just outside, and an impromptu news conference took shape. Questions began with ones that were pretty much expected.

"How did you do it? Is there a special math/statistics formula? And what about the Gardner-Webb games? How in the world did you know that they would beat Kentucky then lose to Dayton?"

Then he got a question that shocked him. A female reporter elbowed her way to the front to the group and put a microphone just inches from his face. "Can you tell us if there is any truth to the rumor that you have an eleven-year-old niece who actually picked the teams? We've heard she is some kind of what they call an autistic-savant, a math genius of some kind?"

Cusac's mouth dropped open and he stepped back, bumping up against the door. The crowd took another step forward. One reporter yelled from the back, "Where does she live? When can we talk to her?"

Cusac lowered his shoulder, pushed his way out of the group, and bolted from the press conference. He raced to Cheeky's house where her mother stood just outside her front door, hunched over a chair, in her nightgown, fending off a handful of reporters who demanded to talk to Cheeky. The hospice nurse was imploring Donna to close the door and come back inside.

When she saw Cusac she screamed at him, "What in hell have you done? How did you get us caught in this mess? She's just a little girl!" Cheeky herself was nowhere to be seen. Her mother was disheveled and disorganized. Her hands trembled, and she stumbled as she and Cusac moved back inside the house.

"Get the hell off my property!" Cusac turned back one last time and screamed at the reporters. "I'll have you arrested if you don't leave right now!" Most left, but a few lingered in the road in front of the house, unwilling to fully abandon the rumored story that an eleven-year-old math prodigy had an algorithm for predicting outcomes of basketball games, and now had picked a perfect bracket through the first two rounds of the NCAA tournament. None of the reporters knew, or would say, where the rumor came from, but it had taken on a life of its own. It was the top trending story on social media. As he helped his niece back inside, Cusac said softly to himself in the form of a question. "Rebecca? Did you do this?"

Within the hour, Cusac packed several bags for his charges to relocate to the home of a friend of Cheeky's mother. The friend and her husband both worked as police officers, and they arrived within minutes after they were called.

"No one's getting to her at our place," the uniformed man said emphatically.

Finally settled in this private location, and Cheeky and her mother looking more relaxed, Cusac retreated to a room by himself to look at a long list of cell phone messages he had ignored for the past two hours. Most he did not recognize and were from distant area codes. One call he did recognize, from the professor who was head of the math department. The message, delivered in an uncharacteristically quaking voice, urgently demanded his presence first thing tomorrow in the university president's office. Investigators from the office of the National Association of Collegiate Athletics would be on campus later today. They would need to speak to him about his perfect bracket and his relationships with members of the basketball team.

Cusac sat with his head in his hands. His heart raced. *Is there any way I could have screwed this up more? I've got a dying woman and a little girl freaking out. I made a student crazy. Did I get Roma and Simon in trouble? Is the university in trouble? Are they going to fire me . . . or sue me?* He sank to the floor and stared at the ceiling.

THE CRAZE GOES GLOBAL

N o one in the Consortium war room was familiar with Hazel Grithens, or exactly sure what effect she might have on the contest. As people talked in small groups, some wondered if she was truly some sort of genius who had this all figured out. Most people could not fit that assessment with the person they saw on television. Activity in the room was slowly picking up but a mood of caution and uncertainty reigned.

Sinclair said, musingly, "I'm still trying to figure out the Bloomberg connection."

Alinsky, who until this moment had remained silent, exploded. "Don't see it? Don't see it? Connect the dots! It's right in front of you. This woman is not some humble little house cleaner who got lucky. She's a shyster!" Alinsky strutted around the room, gesturing dramatically and explaining, "This woman has connections and she has money. You got to be connected to get on that television station. More to the point, she's workin' a scam, and she's going to walk away with more money! It doesn't matter if she never picks another winner, she's perfect until the next game, which is when, Thursday? She's got four days to work this scam."

Sinclair's mind raced to keep up with all the new information. She directed her question to Alinsky. "So, how do we handle this? Just wait and hope she picked at least one loser?"

"I don't know. I haven't figured out her game just yet. She may be gold. She may be poison. I think we reach out to her because right now she's got a whole lot of people looking at her. We might be able to ride along on her little fundraiser and raise some funds for us."

A staff member in the corner of the room raised his voice and pointed to the television screen that was turned to ESPN. "He's talking about the second perfect bracket. I think he just said there's this math teacher on some college campus in North Carolina, but they're having trouble getting to him. Wow. Two perfect brackets and both in North Carolina." No one else seemed interested in the second perfect bracket. The buzz about Hazel picked up again and ruled the room.

For the next two days, Hazel Grithens was everywhere in the media. Seemingly out of nowhere, a sophisticated marketing team materialized around her. Again, it was Alinsky who knew the people who knew some other people who knew Hazel's people, so the contact was made. Alinsky brought in his own version of another advertising team, having been now convinced that the whole scheme could work the way Sinclair had envisioned. Alinsky described the arrival of Hazel as jet fuel on an open fire.

At one point in the war room, Sinclair heard Alinsky talking with people she did not know. A heartbeat away from confronting him on what she perceived as his freelancing what was still her baby, Sinclair held her tongue. She decided to trust him, for now, and limited her guidance to making sure that Rod Browning and Marilyn Seale were brought into the loop as Alinsky openly grasped the reins of the advertising part of the project.

However, the Hazel act was not the only bizarre presentation of the advertising tracks brought into play. The tech-savvy youth of

South Korea had already adopted as hero the Korean-born superstar freshman basketball player for the Oklahoma State Cowboys. Jon Park had won his first two tournament games in convincing fashion. Now that Simon Bradley was out of the tournament, Jon Park became the player who received the most airtime from the basketball pundits about his potential as a first-round NBA draft pick.

Facebook, Twitter, and all the other social media traffic about Jon Park was expected. What no one anticipated came late afternoon on Wednesday, the day before the next games. TV screens and every available mobile media venue exploded with an elaborate, stunningly choreographed, Gangsta Rap homage to South Korea's new favorite basketball son.

Somehow in forty-eight hours, Alinsky had managed to gather a remarkable cast of performers on the unused stage of a casino undergoing renovations. Consortium members, and much of the world, watched a dozen fit and talented, young Korean women and an equal number of impressive young men, dance to a loud rap rhythm, all dressed in cowboy and cowgirl outfits in the Oklahoma State school colors. Expertly staged and artfully recorded, highlighting a combination of athletic and sexual appeal, Alinsky sold it to CBS for $9M. His only regret was that he later concluded he sold it cheap. Nike, Coke, Target, and Samsung all managed to buy into CBS's use of the ad and Photoshopped their own products into the youthful joy and exuberance of the dance. The money the other advertisers paid CBS was never disclosed, but the television network made money.

The creative youth of South Korea responded with their own smartphone recordings published on YouTube. The one that got the most play featured a certain regional dictator whose round body morphed into a basketball that was bounced up and down the court, then slam-dunked repeatedly into the basket. The faces of those in the video, men and women who were clearly talented athletes, were creatively replaced with the faces of various world leaders.

In that same forty-eight hours, Rod Browning and Marilyn Seale had been besieged by a score of South Korean companies wanting to buy banner ads to display on the Billion Dollar Bracket website. Their turnaround time would become a story later that summer in *Fortune* magazine, detailing the creation and display of their web advertising using the cloud. The ads took sixteen hours to create, approve, and bring to contract. They ran for three days and earned Sinclair Dane's team a stunning $37.3M. Those who bought ads were pleased because the often-clichéd phrase "the eyes of the world" was made manifest. The number of visits to the Billion Dollar Bracket website would have crashed any physical servers Sinclair Dane could have used. *Fortune* followed with another article in the fall about the genius of cloud computing, the bracket contest being exhibit A.

Toward the end of the day on Wednesday, Alinsky and Sinclair met privately in her office, away from the continuing work in the war room, reviewing all that had happened. For two days, she had gone back and forth between the hospital and the war room, not feeling fully there in either place as the other drew her attention away. She kept asking for updated information on the second perfect bracket, but the information continued to be spotty and inconsistent. The man was clearly hiding out, avoiding all attention.

"This has gone in ways I never, never figured," Sinclair said slowly to Alinsky as she exhaled and slumped her shoulders.

"Yeah, and that's the beauty of it!" Alinsky came back, still exuding energy and excitement in contrast to Sinclair's fatigue. "It just grows and grows! Do you understand what we've got here?"

Sinclair struggled to organize her thoughts: her mother still in the hospital, the roller coaster of coming to trust Alinsky, watching him seize the project, and the two perfect brackets inching forward, either one of them a threat to the project. She looked at Alinsky and managed a smile with her mouth, below sad eyes. Every time she tried to think about contest issues, her mother's face—and injuries—interrupted her thoughts.

A written note lay in front of her, describing the man with the second perfect bracket, but nothing in the material suggested there was anything to do but wait and hope.

"I'm exhausted. I need to sleep. I have to go home." Sinclair said softly, "I'll see you tomorrow." Sinclair drove away, aware that the contest was moving forward at a frenetic pace and that she was exerting little control over what her team was doing. She didn't know whether she was on a fast train to riches or going off the tracks to ruin.

MEN IN BLACK

On Tuesday at ten a.m., two days before the next round of games among the final sixteen teams in the tournament, Cusac walked into a meeting in the university president's office. He had met three of the people in the room: the school's athletic director, the head of the math department, and his student Miles. The university president, whom he had seen but not actually met, soon entered the room and took control of the meeting, introducing two others as investigators from the National Collegiate Athletic Association.

Despite feeling exhausted and overwhelmed by the attention from the bracket contest, plus the stress on Cheeky and her dying mother, Cusac couldn't help but allow himself a smile at the appearance of the two from the NCAA. They were virtually identical twins, sporting black suits; white shirts; and thin, black ties. Each wore some sort of earpiece with a wire leading down into a coat pocket. Both were tall and fit, had short haircuts, and square facial features. Cusac thought quietly to himself that if they put on dark glasses, they would be right out of the movie *Men in Black*.

President Osborne noticed Cusac's smile and made a distinct throat-clearing sound to impart a sense of gravity to the meeting. Cusac glanced at Miles, who gave an undisguised thumbs-up gesture with both hands accompanied by his own smile and a quick nod of his head. All eyes then turned to the president.

"Dr. Cusac, do you know why I have called you to this meeting?"

Cusac remembered the comments from Miles in the Snack Shop about the rules for and scrutiny of athletes by the NCAA. Several thoughts ran through his mind, but he answered honestly, "No, I have no idea." The continued smile and relaxed body language of Miles gave him a sense of reassurance about what might be coming.

The president continued. "Needless to say, all this attention about your recent fame for the bracket contest is, shall we say, noteworthy. However, the fact that you have a relationship with several of the student-athletes who played in the tournament has not escaped the attention of those responsible for the integrity of our institutions, especially as it relates to betting on collegiate sports." Again, clearing his throat, the president gave a quick nod to the two investigators, who returned no acknowledgment of the gesture.

No longer smiling, perceiving the comment as accusatory and insulting, Cusac gave a measured reply, "You are, I suppose, referring to the fact that I teach mathematics to students who are athletes?"

The president continued, speaking in a manner that sounded to Cusac like a prepared speech. "Yes, and when you were hired here, you were clearly instructed that the classes you teach will be—"

Cusac interrupted him, "I do remember my instructions, the understandings, with the Dean, about my role. I think we all know that. So, if there is a question of impropriety here then please state it." Cusac looked, in turn, at all the people in the room. It seemed odd to him that the two investigators again said nothing. The demeanor of the two men in black was neutral and impossible to read.

The president resumed slowly, cautiously, "No one, as far as I know, has accused anyone of anything, but we do have this unusual situation here."

"It is not a logical proposition that one be required to prove innocence regarding a charge that has not been made," Cusac deadpanned. His anger allowed him to disguise his anxiety, but he held his fingers tightly in a fist to hide that they were trembling. With no framework of comparison for this experience and no clues beyond Miles's apparent confidence, he felt a twinge of panic. He wondered if Rebecca could somehow be involved.

"I guess all we want is to hear from you that your relationship with the students has been strictly that of student and teacher, and there has been no stepping outside the boundaries of that relationship."

Cusac parroted the president's words, his voice starting out timid but finishing strong. "My relationship with my students has been strictly that of student and teacher and there has been no . . . crossing of those boundaries. Did I say it right?" He looked around the room. All remained silent. The president scanned the room for reactions. The investigators looked down at their shoes.

"Then I guess we are done here," the president finally spoke. One by one, the people in the room filed out with no comment on what had happened and without formal or even minimally polite goodbyes. The investigators shook hands with Miles, but otherwise left quickly with no comments or interactions with any of the others. Cusac stayed behind and approached President Osborne.

"That's it? That's what I came here for?" Cusac asked, his puzzlement showing in his voice and in his gesture of upturned palms.

The president moved to gather some papers from his desk and motioned with a nod and turn of his head toward the door for Cusac to follow the others outside. He gave a brief comment as Cusac turned to go, "It's just a little dance we do from time to time. Thanks for coming in."

As Cusac left, Miles called to him from a bench just outside the building that housed the president's office. His smile broadened to a grin and, with his arms in the air, flashed a victory sign with both hands. "You were flippin' amazing, Doc. Do you know how flippin' amazing you were?"

"I'll take your word for it, but only if you'll tell me what in the hell just happened."

"Just come with me to the Snack Shop, Doc, and I'll tell you all about it."

Over an early lunch of cheeseburgers and milkshakes, Miles laid out the events that unfolded directly after Monday's class, during the time that Cusac was confronting the reporters and moving his niece and Cheeky to the safe house. The NCAA investigators had arrived at noon at the office of the president, demanding to speak with any or all of the students in Cusac's class.

Miles took his time, relishing his description of what went on during the previous twenty-four hours. "See, they thought they had it all figured out. They were sure your class was clearly a scam, set up to pass the dumb-ass athletes so they could stay eligible. And more, you must have paid off Roma and Simon to lose to Dayton to keep your bracket perfect."

"That makes no sense."

"Let me finish here, Doc," Miles interrupted, somehow able to take a bite out of his burger, laugh, and talk all at the same time. "So, what they did was gather about a dozen of the class, including me, and Roma, even though he wasn't in the class yesterday."

"You mean they got them together for . . . for what?"

"Patience, Doc, patience. I'm telling you this. They also had Bowman in the room. The big football player. The huge guy?"

"The one that never speaks?"

"Right. The one that looks strong as a bull and twice as smart.

See, they figured he was this dumb jock, and they started grilling him on what he was learning in the class."

"That doesn't sound good."

"Oh, yes it does, Doc, yes it does. See, Bowman was actually a plant by the Dean's office. He was only there to make sure you were teaching a real class. Bowman's an honor student majoring in . . . in . . . everything. He's a flippin' genius. And so this investigator starts grillin' him about things. And then Bowman nailed him on something. They got into all this stuff about math concepts, and it turns out one investigator didn't know the difference between the statistical concepts of reliability as distinct from validity, but . . . but . . . and here's where it gets good. The other investigator did know a lot about science and math and the two of them, him and Bowman, start talking about that guy in *A Beautiful Mind*, the math genius? I'm sure you know all about him."

"So, Bowman and the other guy . . . did what?"

"They started talking about something called game theory, and chess, and something called chaos theory. I think that's what they said, or something like that, way over my head. Nobody in the class had the foggiest. They began talking about the Russian guy Gorbachev and Henry Kissinger and the games they played over nuclear weapons. Went on for at least fifteen minutes. And then it was over."

"That was it. The investigators were finished?"

"Totally finished, wrapped it up. Locked it down. These two NCAA guys figured out there was no problem here. They brought us all up here and bought us a late lunch." Miles finished his story with an open hand gesture sweeping around the booth.

"They bought you lunch? They bought the athletes lunch? I thought that was illegal."

"Ain't that something, Doc? You buy Simon Bradley a cheesecake and he's ineligible and the school goes on probation, but the NCAA investigators can buy your entire math class a whole table of burgers and fries."

"What about the part about me fixing the outcomes of the games to fit my bracket?" Cusac added.

"Well, that might have been the funniest part. The dumb guy investigator did bring that up, but the smart guy, the one that Bowman got going with, he knew that was bogus. So, when Bowman said something like if the professor could pay off or do something magical to get Gardner-Webb to beat Kentucky, you weren't just a genius, you'd be at least a wizard if not an out-and-out god, so when he said that we all laughed because we all knew it was over."

"What about Simon? Did they talk to him?"

Miles paused, smiled, and looked down at the table. "Doc, I won't fuss at you for you not understanding all of this, but the fact is, Simon's gone. He left with his parents after the Dayton game and went home to Australia. I watched him sign the papers to hire an agent before he even got back to the locker room. Flashy-dressed-agent guy had been sitting in the stands for every game since the start of the conference tournament, just waiting for Simon's time in college to be over. Do you see it now? Simon was here at Gardner-Webb for one thing and one thing only: to get a professional basketball contract, and when his season was over, he was gone. Split. On to the world of big money. Agent will front him a few $100,000 and make a big profit when Simon signs with the NBA."

"Wow, I guess I should have known that . . . But to not even finish the school year?"

"Doc, he didn't even go back to clean out his dorm room. He texted a guy on his hall saying they could divide up all his clothes and books and stuff. You should have been there in his room later that night. Talk about a feeding frenzy. Everybody wantin' a little piece of the stuff that used to belong to the next great NBA star."

"Okay, Miles, let me see if I've learned something here. I think I'm learning. That first time we met in the Snack Shop, I said something about Roma being Simon's big brother to protect him from the big bad world. Do I need to modify that?"

"Pretty good, Doc, pretty good. You're not hopeless here. But fact is, Roma's job was not to protect Simon from the world, it was to protect Gardner-Webb from Simon Bradley."

"Got it. Simon's going to be a millionaire regardless, but the school didn't want to have to pay some of the bill for it."

"And they almost did, Doc, they almost did. Want to hear another story?"

"I do, but let me guess something. I think it was at least two times you used the phrase 'something like that' when I asked you a question about Simon. One was about Roma's black eye. Am I warm here?"

"You're smokin' hot, Doc, you do pick up on things. Yes, let me tell you about the black eye. It was Monday night after we won the Big South tournament. Roma, Simon, and me were driving around in my dad's car. I told you I grew up near here, and I can get Dad's car from time to time. Well, Simon gets a phone call and—to make a long story short—we ended up at three in the morning in Shelby at this car dealer's car lot. Car guy was standing there with aforementioned flashy-dressed sports agent who wanted to sign Simon as his client, and they were standing there right beside this brand-new Tesla, and in the passenger seat was this leggy, blonde woman."

"Oh boy." Cusac's eyes grew wide.

"Oh boy, and oh shit, and holy crap. Roma got between Simon and the agent and told Simon: 'Do not take the keys of that car! Do not get in that car! Walk away now!' Simon was beyond reason, looked at the car, looked at Barbie in the car, and popped Roma right in the face."

"So, does that mean Gardner-Webb could still be in trouble?"

"Actually, it turned out okay. Roma picked up a two-foot-long steel pipe lying on the ground next to the fence, and he used it to take out the right front headlight of the Tesla. When he moved on to the other one, the agent and the car guy recalculated the cost of the transaction and got the hell out of there. Simon took a few hours to calm down but ended up thanking Roma. That night could have ended way worse than it did."

Cusac and Miles grew silent and took a few bites of their burgers, both believing the topic was exhausted. Cusac spoke, "So, here we are. The school is safe. Simon is already a legend. What about you?"

"I got a pretty good shot at law school, if I can figure out how to pay for it. Looks like a lot of debt in my future in addition to what I have already." Miles's eyes grew wide. "But what about you, Doc? You still got a perfect bracket after two rounds. Think you'll make it all the way? Hey, here's an idea. Roma and me and one of the assistant track coaches are throwing a little party Friday night to watch the games. Second day of the Sweet Sixteen. Want to come? You'll be the guest of honor."

Cusac considered the invitation for a moment, then remembered what he had waiting with his niece and Cheeky. The hospice nurse told him that Donna had only weeks to live, at best. He needed to spend as much time with Cheeky as possible.

He gave a tactful refusal of the invitation, and the two said their goodbyes. As he walked out of the Snack Shop, he reviewed some of the things he learned from the hospice nurse, and from Davida Thompson. He reassured himself that he was not in this alone. Each step home alternated between confidence and dread for what he would face.

HAZEL'S FUNDRAISER

By Thursday and through Friday, Sinclair had made peace with the need to direct the greater share of her time and attention to the needs of her mother. From the hospital room, she checked in once or twice daily with her team and received reassurance that things were under control at the Consortium. She and her mother both slept for most of the two days, Sinclair in a reclining chair beside her.

Sinclair did turn on the hospital room television enough to catch some of the color commentary for the college basketball tournament that came to be known as March Madness, how it had for years generated many parties and gatherings where friends, families, and office-mates crowded around big TV screens to cheer for their favorite teams. Sinclair wondered if Hazel Grithens ever took part in such ritual. What was certain is that both Hazel and the secretive professor at the small North Carolina school had predicted the winners of the first forty-eight games of the tournament, and that this garnered the attention of a great many people.

Amazed, Sinclair watched the Hazel Grithens part of the story glean most of the airtime for the off-court coverage. ESPN came on board for creating a spectacle, the purpose of which was for Hazel to raise money for several historically black colleges and universities throughout the South, but primarily in North Carolina.

ESPN agreed to cover the telethon event that would take place during the games on Friday, and cut away from the games to cover the event, as long as her bracket stayed perfect.

Certainly, everyone would make money, including ESPN through its traditional advertisers, but who could argue with the charitable cause that Hazel had set in motion? She continued to present herself as giving away money, by investing in the processes that created the machinery of the telethon event.

Sinclair was watching on Thursday when Hazel opened up her event in the Carolina Theater in Durham, North Carolina. A modest-sized stage area provided room for a variety of "celebrities," who turned out to be mostly college administrators and sports coaches, almost exclusively from the ranks of the schools who would benefit. Phone banks dotted the stage and filled the side aisles of the theater to take donations and pledges.

But the real celebrity was Hazel. She took the stage wearing a long, white robe, her head adorned with a decoration that seemed like a cross between an African head wrap and a traditional British crown. Two assistants, men dressed in white suits and wearing headset microphones, moved quickly across the stage introducing the guests.

The most bizarre, and clearly the most attention-grabbing part of the fundraiser, came when Hazel and her assistants came forward with glistening white ceramic bowls and pitchers of water and began to wash the feet of her guests. She seated them one by one before her in a large, throne-like, ornate chair and ceremoniously removed their shoes and socks to begin the cleansing. A few were taken aback, clearly uncomfortable with this unanticipated intimacy, but others seemed moved, as if in a religious service. At the completion of each washing, Hazel pronounced a sing-song, chant-like blessing, "Go forth, soldier of God, your feet have been washed by a child of God, and you are truly touched by His hand." When the washing was complete, the shoes of each guest were replaced with new Nike basketball shoes.

Watching all this unfold, Sinclair first wondered if she was dreaming. She struggled to make sense of what was happening, how her contest had turned in such a bizarre manner, and what this meant to the revenues. Sinclair muted the sound. She picked up her phone to call someone back at the war room, then realized she had no specific question to ask. She turned off the television, rose, and walked to her mother's side. Lillian Dane was sleeping peacefully, thanks to pain pills. Sinclair returned to her cot and to sleep.

Sinclair learned only later that Hazel's bracket stayed perfect for the first of the two games, and for that several-hour period of time, money flowed in. As the chance for victory in game two slipped away, Hazel redoubled her efforts to encourage donations and pledges. She scolded the viewership, suggesting her team was losing because people were not giving generously enough.

Hazel's telethon raised enough money to write a check for $21M, split between six historically black colleges and universities. Due to the contract that Alinsky's people negotiated with Hazel's people, the Consortium earned $5M.

REBELLION

On Saturday, Lilith and her team took a break from the war room and gathered in her two-room apartment to eat pizza and watch several of the games that would decide the final four teams. Twelve people, some of whom were knowledgeable about basketball, others who were there for the company, clustered around a small television. The play-by-play of the game gave way at times to reports on the bracket contest, with some attention to guesstimates about how much money it was bringing in for the Consortium.

A woman sitting behind Lilith steered the conversation away from basketball talk. "Does anybody besides me think we're underpaid? I mean, we're bringing in a ton of money, more than I think they thought we would."

Lilith responded, seated between two other women on her small couch. "Well, I just hoped to get enough to get my teeth fixed." She flashed a grimace of a smile to first the woman on her left, then to her right, showing teeth with a half dozen gaps in upper and lower crooked teeth. "I hate having to hide my mouth. You know what it would cost to fix these teeth? $10,000, at least."

A tall, red-haired man stroked his scruffy beard and put in, "Well, I make more doing this than delivering pizza, but not by much."

Another man added, "I'd be doing Uber, if I had a car that ran."

The woman who started the conversation weighed in again. "Do you see what we're watching here? These big ole giant man-boys playing a child's game that earns them money for college and, for some of them, pro contracts. I say again, what about all the money we're makin' for Snow White and the three boomers?" "Hey," Lilith interrupted, "Sinclair's not so bad. I bet if we approached her in the right way, she'd think about giving us a little more."

"Well, that's a great idea. You do it. We hereby nominate you to go to the boss and get us more money. We'll all stay home Monday and not come in 'till the contract's rewritten." Lilith looked around the room and saw everyone nodding assent. She agreed to do it.

Early Monday morning, after the weekend that reduced the number of teams from sixteen to four, Rod Browning's advertising staff huddled with several of Marilyn Seale's social media team around the largest of the computer monitors in the Consortium war room. The defined task of the group was to understand how the outcome of the weekend's games would affect their ongoing efforts. A pair of twenty-something men from Marilyn's shop, self-identified as basketball fanatics, took turns giving their opinions.

"Okay, Jon Park's Cowboys—that's Oklahoma State—are gone, so my guess is that South Korea won't be as interested the rest of the way," offered the more athletic-looking man of the two.

The nerdy-looking guy answered, "Right, but we're still two for three with the foreign connection. Xavier still has the Russian guy, and we still have the Chinese twins who play for St. John. Even better, they won't play each other until the championship game, if they go that far. So, we could have all three of them in games throughout. That's the jackpot for the international options."

Marilyn weighed in as Rod nodded his agreement with her,

"Wow, I'm totally lost with the basketball stuff. How do you guys keep up with all the players on the different teams?"

The two younger men simply smiled at each other. A young woman from the larger group put in, "They live it and breathe it. Even if there was no $1B contest, they'd still be wallowing in it, but let's focus here, it's about targeting the market, isn't it?"

"It's absolutely about targeting the market," Marilyn regained control of the conversation. "So, let's make a plan. You two, and anyone else who is that much into who is still who in the competition, make a detailed list. Give us a rundown on where these teams come from, what kind of cities and markets they represent. Where is St. John located anyway? And Xavier? What town is that in? I do know the next games are Saturday, and it's just Monday, so we have some time to push this full-speed ahead."

"Actually, the time frame is pretty generous," added Rod. "If I can get that list about markets by the end of today, I can have banner ads for the website ready to go by tomorrow. And with the experience we've developed so far, and the contacts we've developed, I think we've got a lot of room to run."

"You know what else you have, don't you?" asked one of the young men.

Marilyn and Rod looked puzzled.

"We're done with Hazel and her show, and that's a relief, but we still have one perfect bracket. Is no one going to talk about that? That mystery guy in North Carolina is still perfect."

"Uh, yeah. I knew that. That's important," Rod replied softly. Muffled, nervous laughter filled the room.

After a short pause, Marilyn broke the silence. "By the way, I don't see Lilith here. Is she coming in today? Can we call her?" Marilyn then realized that only two of the staff that she placed under the direct supervision of Lilith had come in.

Sinclair's mother, Lillian, underwent a second set of surgeries to realign a broken arm and finger. Sinclair stayed with her and used the time in the hospital to develop a useful communication with her doctors, talking them into secretly medicating Lillian for her psychiatric condition, essentially skipping the conversations with the patient herself. In a matter of just a few days, Sinclair's mother became more calm and thoughtful, and communicated more easily. Although encouraged, Sinclair felt pulled from two sides, the first being the hope to have rational conversations with her mother and perhaps get her to accept the apartment living arrangement. The other pull came from the Billion Dollar Bracket war room. She had not been back there for several days and was out of touch with the work of her staff.

But by now, Sinclair trusted her team and was less suspicious of Alinsky, so she let them know to keep her informed as needed and bother her only with vital issues. They did keep her informed, about almost everything. They did not tell her that with three games yet to be played, there was still one perfect bracket by the math professor in North Carolina. And they didn't tell her about the mini rebellion that erupted with a key part of the staff.

Lilith arrived later that morning, armed with a written proposal for an increase in compensation for her team, based on the level of money earned by the Consortium. When she found that Sinclair was not there, she almost backed out of the plan. But she knew the team was waiting for a call, so she approached Marilyn with the idea.

Alinsky arrived just after Lilith had presented her crew's demand for a new contract to Marilyn. He quickly inserted himself into their hallway conversation. Marilyn looked stunned and struggled to respond to the demands put forth in Lilith's new proposal. Alinsky listened, deferring to Marilyn, and waited until he was convinced their conversation was going nowhere. He then gently took control of the negotiation. "Mind if I jump in here?" he asked politely.

Neither Marilyn nor Lilith responded definitively to Alinsky, but their silence seemed to him to be a form of consent. He walked closer to them, touched each on the elbow, and ushered them into Sinclair's private office away from the war room. He settled himself into Sinclair's chair and motioned for them to take their seats opposite him. Neither Marilyn nor Lilith had been in Sinclair's private office, and both seemed a little uncertain but followed his lead.

Alinsky continued. "Young lady, if I understand correctly, your proposal contends that, due to the unexpected success of our enterprise and the vital role you play in it, you deserve compensation beyond the original contractual agreements." His tone was direct and professional, showing neither sarcasm nor implied judgement.

Lilith, unsure if Alinsky's question was a rebuke or something more positive, hesitated before giving an answer, then she nodded, almost imperceptibly, and said, "I think that is an accurate statement."

Alinsky turned to Marilyn, maintaining an unemotional stance. "So, how long would it take to recruit and train replacements for her and for the others?"

Marilyn's face showed a combination of panic and bewilderment. "We can't—I mean, we can, but it would take—no, the games would be over by the time we—or at least we'd lose two or three days, most of the week, of prime ad days. I don't think we could do it, really."

Alinsky turned back to Lilith. "So, young lady, just for the sake of argument, if I put a proposal to you, essentially to accept your offer to keep your crew and even add to it, say, bring in a half-dozen or even more, how many people do you know, like yourself, and like the others you lead—how many more people that can do what you do could you get in here by tomorrow morning or by the afternoon at the latest?"

"You want a Twitter army? I can get you one if you want one." Lilith smiled, then added, "If you've got the money." She realized for the first time that this might work, but worried that she was being too aggressive, even sarcastic, and told herself silently to keep that under control.

"How much were we paying you, up to now?" Alinsky posed his question, as before, with no show of emotion.

"Forty-five dollars an hour, for them. Seventy-five for me." Lilith replied as she shook her head slowly and cautiously, conscious that she was showing disapproval of that number, but unsure how far she could push it.

"And how much did you say you are asking?" Alinsky kept his matter-of-fact, all-business demeanor. He slumped his shoulders and settled lower in his seat, consciously trying to look non-threatening, not wanting to intimidate her, but kept his gaze fixed on her face. She looked down for just a moment before she replied.

"Three hundred and seventy-five. For everybody. Including me." Alinsky heard just the hint of a hesitation and a quiver in her voice as she spoke her number, but she recovered, taking a deep breath, adding, "Still, a drop in the bucket to what you guys are earning on all this. If you want us, that's my number." She lifted her shoulders and sat higher in her seat. He raised up in turn, matching her posture, heads at the same level.

Alinsky smiled as he responded. "Okay, here's *my* number. It's a yes on the number for your team, but not for you. My number for you is $5,000 an hour, up to thirty total hours for the rest of this week, between tomorrow morning and Saturday noon. But here's the catch, or rather the first catch. I want you to spend a good bit of that money, and gear up to do it using the rest of today, for finding more people for your team. You decide what to pay them, the new ones. You decide how many. The amount you don't pay them out of your $5,000, you keep."

Scribbling numbers on a yellow pad in her lap, taking her time before she spoke, Lilith then came back. "So, what's to keep me from just lowballing the number of people I could get and just pocket the money?"

"Because you're not stupid, and because here's the second catch. Actually, it's not a catch, it's an opportunity—sometimes that's the same thing—for every dollar of new advertising we bring in between Tuesday and the end of this, you get a penny. You don't need to do the figuring; I'll do it for you. If we get another $1M in ads, you get $10,000. But I think we will do better than that. Ten times better, maybe."

For the first time in the conversation, Lilith found herself overwhelmed. She sat speechless, trying to fully grasp the implications of the offer. She realized that, despite the time she had spent in the war room with Alinsky, she had never really looked at him closely. Now they looked at each other face to face. He seemed to her so much older than all the people in her world. What was he? Eighty years old, or older? She tried to decide if someone that old should be trusted. What about that expensive suit and tie? She knew approximately what those things cost, even though no one in her life wore such clothes.

Alinsky gave her a moment to think as he directed a question to Rod Browning, who had just then come into the room and taken the last available chair in Sinclair's small office. "So, what do you think, Mr. Browning? Are we going to get more advertising?"

Moving forward in his chair and speaking quickly, with only a bit of fluster and stutter in his voice, Rod replied, "Uh, yeah. We'll get some. Maybe a lot. But how much we get depends on how well we can close a deal with the people we have potentially lined up, convince them that the contest stays on the minds of people who use social media. You do know we still have one perfect bracket, don't you? I've already had some conversations with a few people that have bought from us already, and it's good. They love the perfect bracket angle. But how good? I don't know."

Restrained in his demeanor up to that point, Alinsky exploded with his response, standing up and prancing around the room, circling the table with waving hands and a facial gesture that conveyed astonishment. "Wow. We've got tomorrow's basketball superheroes from Russia and China flying all over the Internet, a world of Russian and Chinese young people hungry to 'be like Mike.' What else do we need . . . other than a little Twitter cyber-force?"

Lilith spoke quietly. "I'll get your army. You have a deal."

"Actually, there is one more catch," Alinsky came back, returning to his seat, pulling his chair closer to her, looking directly into her eyes. "If that guy in North Carolina comes through with a perfect bracket, I can't pay you for the new contract. I'll pay you and the others out of my own pocket, at the original forty-five and seventy-five an hour, but that's just the way it works. You came in with your very creative entrepreneurial gambit, and I like it. Make no mistake, I like the way you think. But you took a risk for a big reward, and now your risk continues. Double or nothin', triple or nothin'. It's the difference between takin' your cash home or rollin' the dice again. Nothin's free. Nothin's easy. No such thing as a sure bet. That's the only way it can work."

Lilith grew quiet. She felt unsettled and intimidated by his direct gaze. Her mind raced; she wondered if he was scrutinizing and passing judgement on her tattoos and her piercings.

Alinsky did not allow her to hesitate for very long. "What's it gonna be, young lady? Time to make up your mind. I've got grandchildren up on the lake that I could be spending time with, but I'm here with you, trying to make you enough money to actually start yourself a retirement fund. Do we have a deal? The rest of us can just walk away now and be rich, but you can't win if you're not in."

"We have a deal," came her soft reply. "I still have a few questions about how I can actually spend the $5,000 an hour, but whatever. We can work it out."

Marilyn Seale, who had grown quiet during the talks between Alinsky and Lilith, jumped back in. "Don't you think we need to clear this with Sinclair?"

"No. Leave her alone. I'll pay for this out of my pocket if $30M isn't enough of a payday for the boss. Actually, give her a call and tell her we had a meeting and everything is going great. Tell her to stay with her mother. Tell her everything's under control."

Marilyn then asked, "Do we tell her that, with three games to go, we still have one perfect bracket?"

"No!" barked Alinsky. The others grew silent. Each looked at the other as if there was more to say. Alinsky flashed a faux smile. Rod and Marilyn had no response.

Lilith excused herself and left the room. "I've got work to do."

Marilyn took a deep breath and reminded Rod and Alinsky, "There is still one perfect bracket and only three games to go."

Alinsky smiled and added softly, "And that's why the two of you'd better get busy. The world is going to be looking at us, and just going crazy about somebody picking a perfect bracket. We have a once-in-a-lifetime opportunity here, and you need to see it clearly for what it is. You need to trust me on this and get to work. We're going to sell more ads and make more money than you ever imagined. I'll take care of anything that you're worried about."

Marilyn's Monday afternoon call to Sinclair interrupted a promising but inconclusive conversation with her mother. Lillian Dane was at least talking about going to the apartment that her daughter had waiting for her. A nurse and a social worker had just left the room after trying to explain details to Lillian. Sinclair felt they were on the right track but that her mother might be a little overwhelmed by so many people talking to her.

Sinclair answered the phone call with her words pouring out hurriedly. "I've got just a minute to talk. I'm working on something here at the hospital, so what's going on?"

"Well, if you've got just a minute to talk?" Marilyn replied cautiously.

"Yes, just a minute."

"Okay, actually things are going well. Uh, Rod thinks we've still got some advertising room to run; with the teams still in it, the, uh, international interest is still there. I can give you the details if you want them."

"No. That can wait. Do you have anything I need to take care of? Is Alinsky around? Any real problems?"

"No. No, I can hear you're busy. So, I'll just say it's all fine. Alinsky's here. Everybody's working together. I'll call you if anything changes, but this should be a quiet few days. Next game is Saturday."

Sinclair hung up quickly and turned back to her mother, who was nodding off again from the effects of pain medicine. Sitting back down into her recliner, she felt optimism for the first time in weeks, with the news from the Consortium all good and the plan for her mother hopeful.

THE WEEK BEFORE
THE FINAL FOUR

Cusac's attention was increasingly dominated by events with Cheeky. The week before the last of the tournament games was not a good one for Cheeky's mother, Donna. The combination of cancer and treatment for it took away Donna's appetite, energy, and mental clarity. On Wednesday, an emergency room assessment raised the possibility of there being blood clots throughout her body. After an overnight stay, the doctors concluded that any treatment options would just as likely make things worse. They decided against even performing further diagnostic tests. Donna returned home to die. Hospice increased the level of service she would receive.

By Friday morning, Donna, Cheeky, and Cusac returned to Donna's home from where they were in hiding with the friends in Shelby. They were alone except for a nurse sitting watch over the deathly ill woman in her bed, and a police officer just outside the door to keep away intrusive reporters. Even with the security, he felt anxious about the aggressiveness he had seen in some reporters. Cusac's perfect bracket was still alive, and no one as of yet had scored an interview with the genius who stood to win $1B with three more correct choices. Cusac stepped outside for a long conversation with the police officer. He gave further instructions about any visitors, thanked him, and came back inside. He moved to sit beside Cheeky, who was busy looking at a book.

"Cheeky, I need to ask you a question."

"Uh-huh?"

"I just want to talk one more time about how much you understand about what is getting ready to happen with your mom."

Cheeky replied without much emotion, "I know she's going away. I know about that. Like my dad went away."

"Yeah, it's kind of like that. Your dad, he lives . . . his house is where, in Ohio, is that right?"

"I dunno."

"Yeah, I think that's right. But his going away and your mother's going away are different. I think your dad lives in a place called Ohio, and he could . . . he might someday come back and see you. I'm not sure about that, but your mother is going away and will not be able to ever come and see you again."

After a brief pause, Cheeky asked a question. "But just *why* do people go away?"

Cusac felt uncomfortable and ineffective in trying to help his grand-niece talk about dying. As he started to speak again, to try to clarify, Cheeky interrupted him.

"Mommy told me that Daddy went away because he didn't want a dumb kid!"

Cusac was stunned and blurted out quickly, "No, I'm sure that's not true."

"That's what my mommy told me!" Cheeky insisted, tears formed in her eyes, and a single droplet rolled down each side of her face.

Cusac struggled for words. He stammered out the best answer he could. "Cheeky, listen to me. I don't know everything, but I've lived a long time, and I've known a lot of people, and what I do know is that when husbands and wives, moms and dads, go apart, away from each other, it doesn't have anything to do with kids. If your dad left for any reason, it was something between him and your mother, and nobody—not your mother or your father—is leaving because of anything about you."

Cheeky stopped crying, looked down at her book, and said, "I don't want to talk about it anymore."

On that same Friday morning that Cusac struggled to talk with Cheeky, Sinclair returned to the war room for the first time in almost a week. Alinsky, Marilyn, and Rod sat with her in her private office to give her a report on all the events of the week. They gave her the good news first, making only a side reference to bringing in a dozen additional staff members under Marilyn's supervision. The three described in celebratory fashion the remarkable growth of advertising revenues driven by the use of social media. They had successfully made their case to prospective clients that there really would be an incredible number of eyes on the ads for their products, if they acted quickly.

Sinclair deferred hearing about the eager new companies in South Korea, China, and Russia that had jumped at the opportunity to ride the perfect bracket craze to worldwide attention and name recognition. She did allow them to bring in the top number-cruncher tech guy on the staff who dramatically displayed the projected revenue estimate from combined entries and advertising. The amount was $463,222,198.

The room fell silent. The tech guy asked if there were any questions. Yes, he was sure about the figures and added that all the advertising revenues were not in and would grow some. Yes, the systems they had in place were handling the flow of money just fine. No, the *Ring-It* application had no trouble being accepted by banks around the world. Then he left.

Sinclair spoke one word. "How?"

Rod and Marilyn began a description of how the payment application, *Ring-it*, was one key. The world was ready for a new player in the online payment systems, and *Ring-it*, based in India but presenting an international face to the world, came along at just the right time. They had start-up money to spend on advertising. They had a product that worked, and leadership that understood that success depended on working quickly, making decisions without thinking them to death. They fully bought into the concept of the quest for the perfect bracket and rode the wave to worldwide attention.

Alinsky interrupted. "When you two are finished with the high-fives, we need to talk about the little fly in the ointment."

"What fly in the ointment?" Sinclair's face wrinkled as she stared at Alinsky.

Marilyn and Rod looked down and allowed Alinsky to take the lead. "We still got the guy in North Carolina sittin' on a perfect bracket. We have three more games, two on Saturday and one on Monday night."

Having held her composure through the roller coaster of the contest, and the events that played out around her mother, Sinclair had now reached the limits of her emotional restraint. She stammered out her response through her tears. "What are you telling me? What in hell? We get all this right . . . and raise over $400M . . . and we might have to give it all back? I didn't . . . we can't . . . how do we . . . ?" She became silent and put her head in her hands and wept.

Alinsky looked at Rod and Marilyn and said, "This conversation might go a little better if I could have some privacy." The two others were happy to leave the room. Alinsky walked to the window and opened the blinds that were two-thirds closed, rearranged several decorative items on the window sill, and cleaned a smudge from window glass, giving Sinclair the time she needed to steady herself.

Embarrassed by her breakdown, but now composed, she asked, "So, what do we do now?"

Alinsky smiled. "Do you trust me?"

"What . . . do I what?"

"Do you trust me?"

Not willing to reveal to him the struggle she had gone through to be able to trust him, she answered the question with a question, "Is there any reason I shouldn't?"

"Ha!" Alinsky blurted out, and immediately changed the tone and the spirit of the conversation. Standing up and pacing; virtually strutting around the room; speaking in a rapid, dramatic manner; rubbing his hands together; then brushing back his remaining, tastefully colored but thinning hair; he spoke directly into her face. "No. There isn't any reason you shouldn't trust me, and I'll give you a few good reasons why you should. You don't even know it, but I've saved your butt a couple of times now."

Back on both emotional feet, Sinclair rose from her chair to look him directly in the face, pulling herself up to her full height so that she actually looked down at him in order to make eye contact. "Okay, there was the reinsurance money. What else?"

Alinsky turned away, paced, and spoke rapidly. "Your advertising people. You know it's a good thing I stayed here as much as I did. Every time I turned around; they were puttin' the letters N-C-A-A on all the ads they were cookin' up. If they would've put just one of them online, we would've had a team of lawyers on our asses, and it would have cost us a pretty penny just to defend ourselves. We are *not* licensed by the National Collegiate Athletic Association."

"I understand the licensing thing, but you've mentioned NCAA before. How is that such a big deal?"

Alinsky rubbed his hands together enthusiastically and licked his lips, clearly happy to be asked about this issue. He then took Sinclair's hand and steered her back to sit on the couch. He pulled up a chair in order to sit so that his head was at the same level as hers. "Have you ever heard of Jerry Tarkanian?"

"I have. Was he a coach?"

"In the 1990s, he had these great UNLV teams, the Runnin' Rebs, legendary teams, legendary coach. He was a friend of mine. The NCAA tried to make him some sort of master criminal. Sure, he didn't always dot the *I*s and cross the *T*s, but it was always some little thing and always about helping out a kid. He loved his kids, and not just 'cause they made him rich—and they did, mind you— he loved those young men. And the NCAA came down on him like the hounds from hell. Maybe it was the proximity to Vegas—I don't know—but they made his life miserable."

"Yeah, but you know that's the way I kinda think of him," said Sinclair. "Corrupt."

Alinsky exploded. "Corrupt? Corrupt! You want corrupt? This makes me go crazy. The most corrupt teams and program in history were those 1960s to '70s UCLA teams. NCAA never even looked at 'em. Because they were connected. Connected! They were never investigated and all those players had cars, apartments, spending accounts, and all this other stuff. It was a scam. It was a scandal! And then they go after Jerry Tarkanian like he was the Mafia's own devil."

Alinsky was back up, pacing and gesturing wildly as he talked. "One more thing, and I'll shut up. One more story, and I can't say this one was true for sure, but it's a story that was told. You know what they wanted to fine him for? For using the wrong ladders to cut down the nets after they won a championship. They had this licensing deal with a company that made ladders, and when you won the championship you had to use the right ladders to cut down the nets. He used the wrong ladders. The wrong ladders! Okay, I'll shut up now. But that's the NCAA. You know it's hard for me to even watch the games. And another thing, when I see these millionaire coaches huggin' on and lovin' on the big old boy players like they were some sort of treasured son, it makes me wanna throw up. I guess they do love 'em. These boys made them all millionaires. I'd hug on 'em too if they got me a $1M raise for winning a championship. The damn money is just so much. It's out of control. Everybody gets the money except the players. But that's another story. I'm done now."

Alinsky took his seat again across from Sinclair. After a brief silence, she spoke. "So, I guess that brings us back to the money *we* are trying to hold on to."

"Actually, it brings us back to the question we started with. Do you trust me?"

Sinclair answered with no hesitation, "I guess I'll trust you."

"Then go on back to the hospital and be with your mother. Everything will be fine."

Sinclair stopped herself from asking how and why everything would be fine. She agreed to let him be in charge while she worked through the weekend on the arrangements for her mother. As Alinsky walked her to her car, he added one final comment. "Oh, and you know that girl in charge of the tweeters and all that? The one with the tattoos and the metal in her nose and her ears and god knows where else? I increased her consultation rate to $5,000 an hour."

"You *what?*" Sinclair gasped.

As he walked away without turning back, Alinsky barked, "You said you'll trust me."

BEGINNINGS AND ENDINGS

Sinclair returned to the hospital room to find her mother out of bed, sitting in the chair that she herself had occupied for the last several days. Amazed at how healthy and alert her mother appeared, she stopped in the middle of the room, not sure what to say.

Lillian Dane pulled herself up to her full sitting posture and announced with a tone of authority, "I'm done with that bed. Beds are for sleeping at night or for sick people. It's broad daylight outside and I'm not sick."

"Well, since you're in the only chair in the room, maybe I'll just perch on the side of the bed here." Sinclair took a position close to where her mother was sitting. The two women regarded each other for the better part of a minute. The mother finally spoke first.

"But I have decided that if I'm going to that apartment you're fixin' up for me, I have one condition."

Sinclair's spirits sank. She steeled herself for another one of her mother's impossible demands, usually something bizarre, usually following from a paranoid fear, and with conditions that could never be met. A sense of gloom swept over her, anticipating the argument that would inevitably lead to her mother's return to the street life. She asked softly, "What is it, Mother? What is your one condition?"

"You have to let me start calling you Clair again. Or I won't go." Lillian's tone was dead serious and she leaned forward in her chair, raising a hand to keep her daughter from speaking. "I know you like that name your father gave you, God knows why. And when you started growing up, you told me to stop calling you Clair. You said that your name was Sinclair and how that was such a serious name, not a fluffy, girlie name. But I like Clair, and I don't like that name he gave you. It was entirely his idea, and when he got something in his head it was his way or nothin' at all. Do you know where he is? Where the old jerk is now, Clair?"

Sinclair was so relieved at her mother's request that she was close to tears. She took a deep breath and gave back a soft reply, "You can call me Clair, Mother. But only you. I like Clair when you call me Clair." She cautiously reached out and took her mother's hand. Both squeezed the hand of the other, and Lillian pumped it up and down a few beats before releasing it. She turned and silently looked out the window.

"I think I know where Dad lives, Mother, but I haven't talked with him in a couple of years. He said I could call him in an emergency, but I haven't called him for anything."

Lillian looked back at her daughter and spoke softly. "That's good, Clair. You were always good at taking care of yourself. You don't need to call him on my account. By the way, I don't know if you've told me about whether you have a boyfriend now. Is there any news about that?"

"No news, Mother, but I think we will have a lot of other things to talk about. We have a lot to catch up on." Sinclair felt a surge of excitement that immediately turned to fear. She had been at this point with her mother many times before. The pull from the street always won. The next few days would show whether it was different this time.

Late Saturday afternoon, only hours before the two semifinal basketball games for the NCAA Championship, Cheeky's mother passed away at home in her bed. The hospice nurse had accurately predicted the time of her death, almost to the hour. Two of Donna's women friends from her church were at the home along with Cheeky's teacher, Ms. Thompson. They sat in the living room with Cusac and Cheeky while the EMT personnel prepared Donna's body for transport. They failed at several attempts to have Cheeky leave the house so she would not see her mother taken from her room. Cheeky insisted that she was not going to leave her mother.

All the adults in the room were surprised when Cheeky had no observable response as the EMT team wheeled the draped cot through the room and outside to the ambulance. The two friends from church stayed another thirty uneventful minutes, mostly filled with small talk, then excused themselves and left, telling Cheeky they would be seeing her again soon.

Cusac happily accepted Ms. Thompson's offer to stay through dinner. As they were starting food preparation, with Cheeky looking through a book at the kitchen table, the doorbell rang. Ms. Thompson rose and greeted a special delivery mailman at the door, then called out to Cusac that his signature was required for a package. "Just some work stuff," he commented to her as he stepped quickly to the front of the house to sign for the thick envelope. Cusac then laid the package aside on a small side table in the hallway.

When Cusac had gone to the door, the two adults had left Cheeky alone in the kitchen, the first time she had even been alone all day. Cheeky ran screaming to them in the hallway, "Are you going away too?" She burst into tears. Ms. Thompson quickly kneeled in front of the terrified child and enfolded her with her arms.

Even with reassurances from both, Cheeky continued to cry and would not be consoled. "Mommy went away. She went away! I hate her. I hate her! And now you go away. Mommy went away. She didn't love me. Daddy went away. He didn't want a dumb kid. I hate Mommy. I hate Daddy."

After repeated reassurances, Cheeky calmed and agreed to sit between the adults on the couch in the living room. She cried, "Mommy didn't love me; she went away. I hate her. Mommy went away. I want my Mommy to come back. Come back!"

Cusac struggled to find the right words, knowing he was fumbling through a situation he did not know how to handle. "You know, Cheeky . . . I don't really think you are right when you said your mother did not love you. I know she did love you. And lots of other people love you. I love you. Ms. Thompson loves you."

"She didn't . . . she didn't act like it. She got sick and stopped lovin' me. She was mean to me. When Daddy went away Mommy stopped lovin' me. That was mean."

Both Ms. Thompson and Cusac sat there, uncertain about what to say, but Cusac understood more of how Cheeky put together the events around her father's leaving and her mother's illness. He spoke. "Okay, I think I understand what you're feeling. But I think I see it a little bit differently. When your mother got left behind by your dad, she probably didn't have as much time to give you love. Because she didn't feel loved by your dad. And then she got sick and didn't have much love to give anybody."

Ms. Thompson added, "It feels really bad to not feel loved." Cheeky responded with more tears but accepted a hand to hold from each of her companions.

The conversation among the three continued into the evening hours with Cheeky becoming incrementally calmer and more peaceful. Eventually, she fell asleep with her head on Cusac's shoulder. Ms. Thompson left the two of them and went into the kitchen to complete preparations for a light meal for the three of them.

After dinner, Cheeky grew quiet and seemed to the others to have no interest in talking more about her mother. Cusac posed a question, "You know Cheeky, I've been thinking about something. Maybe you don't want to talk about this now, but I know you are really good with words. Words that rhyme. I'm not as good as you are with words, but I'm good with numbers. And I know some rhymes that use numbers. So, we have one thing you're good at and one thing I'm good at. Would you like to learn a rhyming game with numbers? Use the thing that you're good at and the thing I'm good at?"

Davida Thompson gave a quick glance to Cusac, conveying that this might not be the right time to bring up something like that, but Cheeky gave an enthusiastic "yes" to the offer. Cusac cleared a coffee table in the center of the living room sitting area and produced some blank printing paper and felt pens. Cheeky happily joined him on the floor around the table.

Cusac wrote the numbers one and two on the first page and said, "One, two, buckle my shoe." Cheeky giggled.

"Three, four, shut the door," Ms. Thompson spoke the words simultaneously with Cusac as he wrote them down.

"Five, six, pick up sticks." Cheeky was fully into the game now, looking back and forth between the numbers Cusac wrote on the paper and then to Cusac as he added the rhyme.

"Seven, eight, lay 'em straight."

"Nine, ten, a big fat hen." With the last rhyme, Cheeky screamed with delight and rolled on the floor repeating "a big fat hen" several times, then added, "Again. Do it again!"

After several more repeats, they decided to try to find new words to rhyme with the numbers, and the game continued with variations.

Once there was a pause in the action, Ms. Thompson stood and spoke. "Cheeky, I do have to go home to my house for the evening. I have to feed my cats. I love my cats. I love you and I love my cats and I need to feed them. Just like we got fed. But if you will let me, I'll come back tomorrow right before I go to church, and then again after church." Cheeky ran to her and hugged her tightly and said that it would be okay to go. While still holding on to Cheeky, Ms. Thompson turned to Cusac and spoke confidently, "I think you got this." Cusac appreciated the vote of confidence but was also happy Ms. Thompson was coming back tomorrow.

BRACKET ON THE BRINK

Cheeky went peacefully to bed an hour or so after Ms. Thompson left. It then occurred to Cusac that one of the two semifinal games for the basketball championship would be over and the other perhaps partially completed. He resisted the urge to turn on the television or computer to see if his bracket was still perfect, deciding he would spare himself the potential stress of a game in progress, especially if his bracket hung in the balance. He concluded he would wait until both games were finished and find out all the information at one time. Looking around the room for a distraction, he picked up the day's newspaper. A soft knock came at the door. Reflecting on the decision he had made to dismiss the police officer earlier in the evening, he had a moment of anxiety about reporters coming back.

Cusac opened the front door to find Miles and Roma Hill. They stood back, hands in their pockets and heads down when he greeted them. Their body language suggested they knew they might be intruding and did not expect to be invited in. Just above a whisper, Miles spoke. "Doc, I know you've got a lot going on, but we just had to come over after that first game, your bracket being busted like that and all. We don't expect to stay, just wanted to say we're sorry. We didn't know if you wanted company or what would be going on. We can leave."

Cusac stood silent before them. The two students saw the glimmer of new information come across his face, realizing that he no longer had a perfect bracket.

Miles and Roma looked at each other. Roma broke the silence, "Oh . . . my . . . God! You didn't know, did you? Wow. We really screwed that one up." He turned back to a red-faced Miles.

"Come on in, guys. I had to hear it sometime," answered Cusac, in a cheerful tone that could have been a response to news that tomorrow would be a nice weather day.

Miles and Roma were still hesitant about coming inside, but Cusac assured them that Cheeky was sleeping, and he wanted some company after a "pretty bad day." He offered them ice water or soft drinks and quipped, "As long as I'm not breaking any NCAA rules." They both accepted ice water, smiled at his joke, and took seats around the kitchen table. Cusac told them about his day, giving equal measure to the distress that Cheeky had shown and to the success of the rhyming games that ended the day. Miles and Roma again apologized for intruding but finally accepted that they were a welcome diversion, even with the outcome of the game.

"I know you didn't pick St. John, Doc, and, fact is, they should not have won that game. I couldn't believe it. They came back from down ten with two minutes to play." Miles gave a brief account of the game that ended the run at the perfect bracket.

"Just have to ask, Dr. Cusac," interrupted Roma. "How did you do it? You got closer to winning it all than anybody. Far as I know, nobody else ever got this far. I know the math skills counted for something, but lots of other smart people have tried to figure it out too."

"Okay, there was some math at work here, along with luck. You guys really want to hear about it?"

Roma and Miles gave wide-eyed head nods that indicated yes.

Cusac opened a folder and pulled out his copy of his form that he had submitted and placed it on the table in front of them. "I kept looking for key variables. Something that reliably predicted the outcomes of games. I never found a perfect one, just too much emotion and too much resting on the expected performance of some very young men. So, what did I come up with? Real simple. Team with the best defense wins most of the time. Information about who has the best defense was not that hard to find. Therefore, after I assumed defensive performance to be the key, and believe it or not, almost every time there was a correlation between good defense plus teams that had older players. Good defense, older players, and of course the original seeding."

Miles frowned, "That's too simple. Can't be the formula."

"Well it's not that simple. I used a progression of variables. Started with the seeding. And usually the better seeded team had better defense and had older players. If all that fit, I picked that team. When it didn't fit is where it got more complicated. Then I rejiggered the data using only the games after January 1, after the early part of the season was over and the younger players had more experience. Then I did it for just the last ten games of the season, weighted those higher, and got a grid that showed a progression of improvement."

"Wow, that's like a mathematical formula for momentum," commented Miles.

"As fancy as that is, Doc, there is one big problem with your formula," put in Roma, "Kentucky against Gardner-Webb don't fit that description. Not seeding. Not older players or defense. We had a crummy defense. We outran and outscored the teams we beat, the direct opposite of your scheme."

Cusac laughed as he replied, "Well, just for fun, and just because I knew I was not going to get a perfect bracket—the odds were just too great—I decided to show some loyalty to the home team. Sort of a throwaway that I thought you would all laugh about. So, how about that? Not exactly dumb luck, but something random."

"What about Dayton? No loyalty for Gardner-Webb against Dayton?" Roma asked.

"Dayton had a first-rate defense. I figured I had proven myself as a loyal Bulldog by then. No way Gardner-Webb was going to get by Dayton, even after Kentucky." All three laughed and then caught themselves, not wanting to wake Cheeky.

Cusac continued. "Actually, I would have picked Dayton over Kentucky. All seniors, third best scoring defense in the whole country, and nobody scored three-point field goals on Dayton. Kentucky was all a bunch of young guys who shot a lot of three-point field goals. But back to Gardner-Webb and Kentucky. In the end it was random events, the injury to the Kentucky point guard and the infamous headbutt that made the difference. No one could have predicted that. And that's why there will never be a perfect bracket."

Having exhausted the topic of bracket prediction, the conversation turned to the futures of the two young men in the room. Roma explained that, similar to Miles, he had his eyes on law school. "North Carolina has two law schools that showed some interest in me . . . but I don't have a dime in my pocket, and my grades are not at the level that they're going to pay my way. Campbell has pretty much told me I could come, but no money for me." Miles added that he had an uncle who said he was going to support him with a loan but wasn't sure that would work out. Both of the students had actually approached Gardner-Webb about staying on in some sort of paid apprentice jobs in university development. Cusac wondered silently whether the school might reward them with a job for their involvement in the Simon Bradley story. In any event, it looked as if both would be spending some time in the work world before law school became realistic.

As the conversation wound down, Roma and Miles stood up together and thanked their host for his hospitality. Cusac returned the gratitude and bid them goodnight. As he closed the door, he stopped in the hallway and picked up the special delivery mail that had come earlier when he and Ms. Thompson were consoling Cheeky. He walked back to the kitchen table, paused to prepare himself another glass of ice water, then sat down and opened the mail he had consciously avoided until now.

KEEPING THE TEAM
TOGETHER

At the same time that Miles, Roma, and Cusac met at the kitchen table on Saturday night, a small residual of the Consortium staff gathered around the war room conference table. What were the implications of St. John's victory that eliminated the remaining perfect bracket? Some staff moved around the room picking up empty cans, discarded paper food containers, and various other items that had accumulated during the weeks that the team had virtually lived in Sinclair's office. Two people lay tightly bundled in their sleeping bags, oblivious to the actions of any of the others.

The group seated at the table included Alinsky and Lilith, who had formed an unlikely but comfortable bond after their negotiations that led to the return of the Twitter army under Lilith's lead. Three of her staff were present along with two from the advertising team. Rod and Marilyn had gone home earlier to attend to their lives beyond the Consortium.

Lilith spoke to the group as Alinsky listened quietly. "Okay, no perfect bracket, but we've still got St. John's Chinese hunky poster-boy twins in the finals, and since Xavier pulled off the other big upset, we still have the Russian guy too. Russia's and China's favorite sons are still in the championship game. That's money. Money in *our* bank."

"Isn't the key item here that we no longer have a perfect bracket?" asked a staffer. "We get to keep all the money, but what's left to get done? And with no perfect bracket, who's going to pay attention to the contest? Isn't the advertising option over?"

"Not necessarily over," explained Lilith. "We still have the avatars making contacts in those countries. We're real active in China and Russia. Lots of action on Facebook and Twitter, so I think there will still be interest in the way the tournament comes out, given all the interest we've generated over the last few weeks. We've linked the main bracket website to a blog with lots of human-interest stories, some of them true. So, people will still have their eyes on us. It's called *ad-ver-ti-sing*." Lilith allowed herself a wicked smile. She looked at Alinsky for confirmation but found him with a puzzled look on his face.

Alinsky asked for clarification. "I have no idea what you're talking about. What do you mean by avatars? And what do you mean by only some of the stories are true?"

Lilith and her team members exchanged glances, and she began an explanation. "Well, it's like this. Each of us, in our little Twitter team here, each have about twenty identities, or avatars, bumping around in the world, including China, South Korea, and Russia, and some in India, all still stirring the pot, stirring up interest in our contest—or I guess now just interest in the games, and some of the players still in it and some not. But I do think the interest goes beyond the bracket contest. We may have created some genuinely new fanatics of American college basketball."

Lilith paused to gauge Alinsky's interest, then continued. "My own personal favorite avatar is Candy. I'm a nineteen-year-old cheerleader for Oklahoma State, and even though my Cowboys lost in the last round, I still keep in touch with my new friends in

Seoul, and some still in Moscow. I have seventeen thousand Twitter followers that are thrilled to know a blonde, sexy but wholesome college kid in the good ole US of A. I have my own share of online marriage proposals."

Alinsky protested. "I thought that kind of thing was illegal, and if it's not, it should be." Lilith's team gave Alinsky a quick tutorial of how social media remained a rapidly changing, truly diverse, and "stunningly creative" place to spend time and express fantasies of what life should be. And it was legal unless the avatar actually committed a crime.

"Tell him about Charlcie," one of the other staffers said to Lilith.

"Charlcie is me, too—actually, a transgender girl who mainly follows the women's tournament, but who got so excited about Stanford's men's team that she filled out a bracket. Stanford didn't last very long, but Charlcie now has fans all over the world. Saudi Arabia was the surprise. Funny, an amazing number of trans people from the Middle East just love basketball, and Charlcie is now their sports guru. And everybody's excited because she's about to get her sex-change surgery."

Alinsky squirmed in his chair and started a question. "Okay, that's a little more than what I want to think about, and I'm a little mixed up about who is real and who is not. But I guess all of this is how—"

"Yes, that's one way how the Billion Dollar Bracket had all those eyes on the website. All that led to the advertising we sold to those companies that do business, or want to do business, in Russia and China, and vice-versa, and et cetera, et cetera, et cetera."

Alinsky had spent enough time in the war room with Lilith's staff that sufficient comfort existed among them for one of her staff to now pose a question to the older man. "Hey, Alinsky, you could have an avatar on social media. What would you like to look like to people in Beijing?" The questioner paused to study Alinsky's reaction, and when he seemed amused, the young man continued. "I could see you as a cross between a young Brad Pitt and Tom Cruise, darker than Pitt, and taller, definitely taller and muscular, like Arnold in the *Terminator*." Laughter filled the room. Another staffer quipped, "What would his name be? Maybe Big Al?" More laughter.

"Now, that should definitely not be legal!" Alinsky responded with mock outrage and a chuckle, then added, "And anyway, what happens when all this is over, do you all have to have stories of how all the avatars die or something?"

"Like I said, it's only illegal if somehow the avatars commit a crime, and when it's over we just delete the accounts. Two months go by, everybody forgets about basketball for a while, and nobody will remember Candy or Charlcie. Things and people move on when you're talking about the online world."

A voice came through the open conference room door. "That's kind of sad, actually."

The group turned to follow Sinclair as she entered the room. The conversation stopped. No one in the room but Alinsky knew the whole story of why Sinclair had been absent from the room for the last few days. Alinsky had kept Lilith and the others exclusively focused on the contest, and everyone was too busy to dwell on their titular leader's absence. Sinclair looked exhausted. Her hair was ruffled and the white shirt under her jacket showed a coffee stain just under her left shirt collar.

Sinclair continued, "So, if I caught the gist of your conversation, we still can push this and expect a return through the end of the games?"

Lilith nodded her assent and added, "Well, it could really fall off over the next two days, but if we can get Marilyn and Rod in here early tomorrow, it's probably worth doing. The final game is Monday night. That gives us a little less than forty-eight hours to work, and we can play the China versus Russia angle with all of our contacts in those countries. We can get a lot of eyes on the website all day Monday and push the advertisers one more time. But we do need Rod and Marilyn."

Sinclair held up her hand to stop the conversation. "I'll call them in a minute, but first, Alinsky, can you and I meet in my office?"

"Only if I can bring my new best friend with me," he came back, gesturing to Lilith.

Sinclair's expression registered her surprise that Alinsky would want Lilith to accompany them, but saw no reason to object and nodded her assent.

Leaving the larger group, Sinclair, Alinsky, and Lilith took seats in the smaller office. Sinclair opened her mouth to speak, then stopped herself, saying that wasn't what she really wanted to talk about. She stumbled over her words and simply stared forward, tears in her eyes. A single tear rolled from her left eye. She didn't bother to wipe it away. After a few seconds she managed to say, "I'm just really tired."

Sinclair knew that neither Lilith or Alinsky knew what she had been through at the hospital. She wondered how much empathy they could have for her tears, and if they saw her as weak. But she saw no sign of disdain or even impatience for her emotionality. Alinsky spoke first, "You don't have to ask anything about the contest. It's all taken care of. Tell us what you've been through."

Sinclair flashed an angry face at Alinsky, opened her mouth to speak, and resumed softly crying. After a full minute of tears, she composed herself. "Of course you're right. I'm in no shape to talk business. I'm a total failure, loser, and all of this is just a farce. I can't even handle my own life, much less all of this." Sinclair clasped her hands together to stop her fingers from shaking.

"Shut your mouth," jabbed Lilith, her soft tone making her command sound like it was meant as a supportive comment. "This whole deal has gone way better than anybody, even you, ever dreamed. You're a fuckin' genius and you don't even know it. Now do what the man said and tell us what's been going on over at the hospital."

"How do you know about the hospital?" Sinclair barked defensively. "What do you know about what's been going on there?"

Lilith continued her gentle tone, trying to be both confrontational but kind. "Give me a break, boss. Everybody on the street knows about your mother and pretty much what happened to her."

"You don't know anything about my mother and me." She lowered her head and folded her arms across her chest.

Alinsky and Lilith both lifted their hands slowly in a defensive gesture meant to calm things down. Sinclair drew inward, silent. A full minute passed. Lilith then spoke again. "Actually, boss, if you'll let me try one more time, and if this doesn't come out right, I'll just shut my mouth and leave. But anyone who's spent any time on the street in Vegas knows who Lillian Dane is."

Sinclair seemed stunned to hear her mother's name but composed herself, realizing that Lilith may have something important to say. "Go on." She said softly.

"Actually, I have two ways that I know about your mother. I know that hospital, good old Montevista, and the psyche ward over there. I spent some time there myself, and to be totally honest about it, I was there with my own mother, both of us hospitalized at the same time, and at the same time that your mother was there. I talked a number of times to your mother. She was . . . is . . . a sweet, classy lady."

"I can't believe that you know—"

"And I know about her from the street. I've never been homeless myself, or my mother either, but more than one of our little tweeters here are people who have hit the streets, or I should say were thrown out on the streets by their asshole families. Your mother was well-known in the places that people go to survive that kind of thing."

Sinclair cried again. "I have done everything I could possibly do to get her off the streets and into a real apartment."

"But some people just prefer the street, I know that too. And you do too. Since you say you've tried all your—"

"And now she's promised one more time to go to the apartment I have for her," said Sinclair, looking up at the ceiling, wiping tears with her fingers, talking chiefly to herself. "And everything will be peachy and we'll all live happily ever after." Her voice trailed off in fatigue and sadness. Neither of the others knew about the other demon with which Sinclair had long struggled: the fear that she too would end up on the street, just like her mother.

Alinsky considered several possible ways to respond to Sinclair, then spoke softly. "Go home, lady. Go home. Sleep. Call me when you are rested. Everything really is fine here. And you will be too. And just for information purposes, the last bracket lost today."

Sinclair showed no apparent response to Alinsky's information, but thanked him for all he had done, and left promptly to go home.

TWO SIDES TO SUCCESS

The following Monday night, the National Collegiate Athletic Association crowned its new basketball champion. The identity of the winner did not matter to Sinclair Dane and her various partners in the Billion Dollar Bracket Contest. Since there was no perfect bracket, she and her group were the real winners. The Consortium team stayed busy through Monday night's final game tracking ads and revenues from their efforts. Sinclair stayed away from the office and the activities of the others, resting and visiting her mother.

Two days after the championship game, on Wednesday morning, a composed and confident Sinclair Dane called to order a full-team update meeting. The four original partners—Sinclair, Alinsky, Rod, and Marilyn—sat at one end of the conference table facing twenty-two staff members who crowded into the remaining space, seated and standing, leaning against the wall, around the packed room. Lilith and Alinsky smiled quick glances at each other, silently celebrating the fact that they had their leader back and in charge.

Each person in the room, other than the original four, upon arrival, had been given a sealed envelope containing a check for bonuses for their work beyond their contractual arrangement. Each envelope was marked: *Do not open until instructed to do so.*

Sinclair gave a general review of the success of the contest but did not disclose to this larger group the full revenues brought in. That figure would wait until the smaller meeting of the original four partners. Sinclair took her time thanking the larger team of advertisers, marketers, and social media specialists, calling out in turn each name of everyone in the room, with help from Lilith. She then asked them to open their envelopes. As the contents were revealed, one gasp after another burst forth, followed by some tears and more than a little laughter. Emotions rippled through the room. None of those who opened the bonus letters expected the six figure checks. More than one recipient asked a version of "is this real?"

Alinsky waited until the emotion in the room died a bit, then gave his prepared remarks. "I, and your leader, Sinclair, know enough about the group of you to know this is probably the biggest check, in one lump sum, that any of you have ever received. Be careful with it. Money can ruin people. Before you spend a penny of it, you better get someone to advise you about taxes. If you don't know anybody like that, I have a little handout that lists some people—none of whom have any business connection to me—and the document I can give you also has a couple of paragraphs about how to pick a good financial adviser."

Alinsky surveyed the room for a response to his offer of this information. None came. He then passed the list of financial advisers around the room. Everyone took a copy. "So, now it is time to say goodbye. A few of you have a little more to do with crunching some numbers. You know who you are, but for now, everybody go on, get out of here. And, in case you didn't hear me before, don't screw up your life because of one big paycheck. Money is dangerous. Trust me on this one."

All rose to leave. Alinsky and Sinclair spoke simultaneously, "Not you, Lilith. You stay."

The meeting continued with the original four partners, plus one. Sinclair addressed Lilith. "So, do you think that group will be satisfied with their bonuses, or will there be another little rebellion because of the amount of money we still have?"

Lilith blushed, paused before answering, then said, "I'm not sure where we are going with this."

"We have a great deal of money left over. What we just gave out is a small fraction of the total take. I don't want anyone to feel cheated with their share. More to the point, I don't want the bother associated with anyone who might make a fuss about feeling cheated."

Alinsky put in, "All were rewarded far beyond their contractual arrangements, so I don't think anyone could successfully mount a real challenge—legally, that is—but we did go through that little readjustment a few weeks ago." Alinsky winked at Lilith and she appeared to relax.

Lilith looked down at the $300,000 check in her hands. "Did everyone here get this kind of money?"

Sinclair replied, "Your check was the biggest, but for some of them, not by a lot. No one got less than half of what you got. And by the way, we still haven't calculated that penny on the dollar thing for the advertising, so you still got some more coming."

"Wow. Now I know why you said that about being careful with money." Lilith took a deep breath and spoke softly, without making eye contact, as if speaking to only herself. "So, that guy with the shaved head . . . the one with the bushy eyebrows? He lives with his parents most of the time. When he has a few good tech gigs in a row, he moves out but usually makes a mess of things. The girl with the red pigtails? She's living in her car now. I don't know what either of them are going to do with $100,000, but I'll tell you this, there's gonna be a lot of weed bought by this group in the next few weeks."

"And so that's not really our problem now," said a frustrated Alinsky. "We just want to know if their problem might become our problem."

Lilith slowly shook her head. "No. I don't believe there will be a problem with any of them. I think they walk away thinking they just got the goose with the golden eggs." She looked around the room. No one offered more questions or comments about the issue of the bonuses.

Lilith stood up to leave. "So, I guess you're done with me now?"

"Nope, not even close," Sinclair barked. "We still have two things to talk to you about. First, you need to hear the final numbers on the revenues."

Looking genuinely surprised, Lilith sat back down. "Okay, I'm game."

Sinclair nodded to Alinsky. "Go ahead, lay it out."

"First, I want to say that my warning about not letting money ruin your life was not just for the kids who just left. Mr. Browning and Ms. Seale, you have the same challenge. I know both of you are successful in your own world. You appear to have managed your business affairs capably before all this. I'll say it more clearly. Mr. Browning, you organized and ran the overall advertising shop in a truly professional manner. Ms. Seale, your guidance for the social media part impressed even me. And I have seldom seen a better partnership in how you two worked together. But, all that said, do you have any idea how much of a check you are going to get?"

Rod Browning and Marilyn Seale glanced at each other and simultaneously shook their heads. Alinsky handed each of the others a single sheet of paper with one number on it, with the notation that this number represented the total profit for the contest. Rod Browning broke the silence as he whisper-read the total. "$831M?"

Alinsky chuckled his reply. "That's a rounded number, but I think it's within one or two percent of the final total. There's still a little more to come in."

"I can't think; my mind is frozen," responded Marilyn. "I was so busy just working on this, I've forgotten what our contracts actually said. I can't begin to figure this out."

"We'll do it for you once the final one or two percent comes in. But you do recall that the two of you didn't want to put assets at risk—you opted for a lesser cut of the revenue—so you won't get a full fourth of the total. Your shares won't be much over a $100M each."

Rod sputtered, "$100M! I can't even count that high. This is ridiculous. It's not possible."

"It's possible, my friend," added Alinsky. "So, let me say it again. People who win the lottery end up broke. Pro athletes who earn millions end up deep in debt. Singers and movie stars are the worst, if they even survive the process. Neither of you are naive, but you need to protect yourself from yourself—and from people who you would never suspect might take you for a ride. Get a good financial adviser, if you don't have one, who deals with this kind of money. Don't go to jail because of the tax man."

Sinclair added that she would be in touch with Rod and Marilyn early next week to wrap up and to answer questions about how to proceed with disbursement of the money. All shook hands. Marilyn and Rod left quietly, speechless.

Silence overtook the three remaining in the room, until Lilith broke it. "I'm not sure why I'm still here. I don't want any more of your money, so if—"

Sinclair interrupted, "We were wondering if you want a job?"

"What kind of job?" Lilith looked in turn at each of the others and added, "And who exactly is 'we'?"

"Well, what I have in mind might take a little to explain. You know a lot about me and my mother, but do you know how that fits with this contest I dreamed up?"

"Not much of a clue."

Sinclair took a deep breath, looked at Alinsky, and continued. "So, the money I get from the contest is my safety net. Pretty much every woman in my family has gone crazy, some more than others. So, I figure I have this time bomb ticking in my brain and could end up like my mother. That's what I fear, even though several shrinks have told me they don't see that happening. Anyway, now I've got enough money to put in place some guard rails to keep me from the streets. And maybe even finally get my mother off the streets. Make sense?" Sinclair added that she had never actually admitted these fears to anyone except her therapist. She didn't try to hide her trembling fingers.

"Makes perfect sense. But I still don't see what that has to do with me and why I'm still in this room."

"Alinsky will take over now and tell you about this job offer, we—I—have for you."

Alinsky jumped in. "There's no 'we' here. This is between the two of you, but I will take credit for coming up with the idea. Here's how I see it. Lillian Dane may go back to that apartment full time or part time or not at all, but chances are that, for now, the streets are her home, or some big part of her world. All I said to Sinclair was, since her mother thinks people are already following her, why don't you get a little murmuration of those street tweeters to actually follow her around and keep an eye on her. Pick out some good people who will cozy up to her. She'd run from the white coats and the dressed-for-success welfare ladies, but a crew of tattooed, fuzzy orange-haired, and unwashed kids might just seem natural to her. Worth a shot."

"And I'd have you run it, Lilith, for a decent salary, and a budget to pay people," added Sinclair.

"So, you want me to be the psych police for your mother?"

Sinclair winced, seeing the skepticism in Lilith's face, but continued her explanation. "Not the psych police, just eyes and ears, and get the information back to me if you see she's in any real danger. If you don't want to do something like that, I understand. I know I'm asking you to do something unusual, and I really don't know how much of your time it would take, or how you'd go about finding and vetting people. But you sure came through with the right people for what we just accomplished. So, I think you can do it. And I trust you."

Alinsky exploded with laughter. "You trust her! Praise heaven! You trust her? Do you know how many times I asked you if you trusted me? And did you ever say yes? Sort of, reluctantly, but not really." Alinsky gradually tempered his laughter to a chuckle and ended with a few faux deep breaths.

Sinclair and Lilith both smiled back at Alinsky. Lilith looked at Sinclair and said, "Your job sounds interesting. I think I could understand it better if we could write something up and use that to talk a little more. Maybe we can work something out."

WHAT NEXT?

At the same time the Consortium held its final meeting, Lewis Cusac walked into the State Employees Credit Union in Shelby, North Carolina. As he sat in the lobby waiting for his appointment time, he took out the thick folder of financial documents he had received in the mail by special delivery last Saturday night. He scanned the final paragraph of the document that started with: "Pursuant to our conversations by telephone . . ." and concluded with: " . . . and in return for this payment, you grant to Mr. Potifar Dillard Alinsky, in its entirety, your claim upon the prize money of the Billion Dollar Bracket Contest."

Cusac looked at the certified check that had been signed by Alinsky two days before the semi-final tournament games, and just to be sure, again counted the zeroes that followed the number twenty-four. Six zeroes. He whispered the words to himself, "$24M for a busted bracket."

His mind raced with what he could do with a trust fund for Cheeky, and how he might help Roma and Miles with law school expenses. Maybe a loan to them that they would pay back with interest, or maybe an agreement that after they start practicing law, they would manage the trust fund for Cheeky when he wasn't around.

The greater part of an hour later, after Cusac was assured that the local Credit Union could handle a $24M deposit, and confirmation that the check was valid, he walked out into a crisp, clear springtime day and said out loud to himself, "Well. How about that."

Alinsky and Sinclair were the last to leave the building after the Consortium meeting. They walked in separate directions to their cars, then Sinclair pivoted and followed him. She called out to him, "Don't you have one more thing to tell me about?"

Alinsky put his car keys back into his pocket and leaned his back against the side of his Lincoln, arms folded across his chest. "I figured you'd learn about it soon enough, but I thought I'd give you a little space to let it soak in. How much do you know and how did you find out?"

"Doesn't matter how I know. Let's just say that when you're talking about a school teacher winning millions of dollars, people find out."

"So, you don't really know how many millions?"

Sinclair took another step to stand directly in front of Alinsky. She raised herself up on tiptoes to exaggerate her greater height and looked down directly in his eyes. "Let's get to the point. When I first heard about this, I asked our bookkeeper if you wrote a multi-million dollar check out of Consortium money. The answer came back negative. So, I figure you bought the professor out with your own money. So, here's the question: were you buying him out for *us* or for *you*?"

Alinsky turned away from Sinclair and put some distance between them. He walked to the front side of his car and braced himself on the fender with his left hand, his right hand on his hip, slowly growling out his reply. "I'm going to do you one more favor and not answer your question right now. But since you made the effort to ask the question, I'll give you some thoughts to help you figure it out."

Sinclair thought for the first time that she had intimidated Alinsky, but he seemed hard to read in the moment. This made her feel cautious. She lowered her eyes and took a step backward to a safe distance away.

Alinsky continued, "You know, for a day or so, everybody was feeling so sorry for the little ole lady Hazel and the frumpy professor guy. Sorry 'cause they lost. Then the word comes out about how they both walked away with a pile of money. Sweet little ole Hazel disappeared the minute her bracket got busted, and yes, she did raise some money for those poor little students. But you can be sure she walked off with her pockets full of cash too. Won't be hearing from her for a while. Her trail's already gone dark. Giving away her money? Hah! She's got more money than God."

Sinclair realized she knew almost nothing about how the telethon turned out, and she immediately felt vulnerable. *How does Alinsky know all this?*

Alinsky picked up the pace of his narrative. "People got this whole winners-and-losers thing all mixed up. You know who the losers are? It's all those people who made you rich. You can say they all only gave you two dollars, but they're losers. Like when people go to a casino. You think people who win jackpots get a better life from it? Hah! The stories I could tell you. Losers! All of them!"

It was Sinclair's turn to lean against the car. She took a deep breath and relaxed, arms down by her side. She decided she'd let Alinsky's tirade burn itself out.

Only a deep breath interrupted Alinsky. "What about me? Am I the big winner? Well, here's the deal. Look at it one way, and I made more money off this than any of you. Look at it another way, and this was my last chance to be a billionaire. Look at it a different way, and I paid that fool teacher $24M for nothin'. For nothin'! And I'm still not a billionaire. I know people who know that about me, and they think I'm a damn loser."

Now in full strut, circling his car, scraping the soles of his feet on the pavement like a bull ready to charge the cape, Alinsky sputtered, stammered, and spit out his diatribe about winners and losers. "And what about you, Miss Sinclair Dane? You're gonna put $200M in your piggybank—and you just might *still* end up on the street. You could *still* end up a loser. And you know why? 'Cause you don't know who to trust, who to thank, and who to walk away from. You know numbers, but you don't know people. I know numbers, and I know people. You need to learn how to know people, and then you won't end up a loser."

At this point, Alinsky had moved to the driver's side of the car, quickly opened the door, got in, and slammed it shut. He started the engine, rolled down the window, and said calmly to Sinclair, "Look, take a little while with this. And when you get to the point that you think it was right to trust me, you give me a call. And we'll talk." He drove slowly away, not waiting for a reply.

Sinclair could have replied. She had her own speech ready to go, but he was gone. She watched him go and then walked to her car. She sat for a moment and reflected on the fact that she was at peace with all he had said. She felt no fear. She told herself she'd have that meeting with him, but she didn't have to decide right then if he was truly to be trusted. Maybe it was more complicated than a simple yes or no.

She pulled her car out of the parking lot and turned toward the hospital. Tomorrow her mother was scheduled to move to the apartment. Her mind raced with possibilities. *Maybe I got myself a couple of new best friends. One's a dwarf and the other's got more tattoos than she has teeth.* As she picked up speed on the freeway, she opened the window of her car and let the wind flow into her face. She smiled, then laughed.

ACKNOWLEDGMENTS

This book is inspired by my love for basketball and is informed by my experiences working as a practicing psychiatrist for forty years.

I played basketball at Gardner-Webb Junior College, now a four-year university, from 1965 to 1967. In 1996, I was inducted into the GWU Sports Hall of Fame, as a 1967 Honorable Mention Junior College All-American.

This book is a work of fiction. Except for the information about Gardner-Webb University once receiving an NCAA probation, a story well-known and widely reported in the general media, the storyline is my creation. Except for the brief reference to Artis Gilmore, who played two years at Gardner-Webb Junior College, 1967-1969, all events and characters are made up.

The work is further influenced by my reading of the book *Indentured: The Inside Story of the Rebellion Against the NCAA* by Joe Nocera.

I would like to thank I. Nelson Rose, Attorney and Professor of Law, Encino, California for his guidance about the legal issues involved in the offering of a gaming contest, the objective of which was to choose a perfect NCAA basketball tournament bracket. If there is any misrepresentation of real-world legal issues in this book, it is entirely my misunderstanding or my choice in the service of creative conflict.

Many thanks to core members of my writing group: Gale, Christy, Lauren, and Robin. Thanks also to Bill Finger for his early reviews of the manuscript.

Many thanks to Terri Leidich and Julie Bromley of BQB Publishers for their hard work and wisdom in bringing the book to print.

ABOUT THE AUTHOR

Drew Bridges is a retired psychiatrist who has restored himself to his default identity of "English major." His restoration included operating a bookstore for seven years in the town of Wake Forest, North Carolina, where he lives with his wife Lauren, a psychotherapist. In *Billion Dollar Bracket*, he draws upon two lifelong passions, the world of college sports and the study of human psychology to create a story filled with suspense and controversy.

His previous novel, *Family in the Mirror,* was selected as finalist in the 2017 Next Generation Indie Book Awards.